Dangerous Liaisons

ROWENA WYLDE

WINSOME BOOKS

The characters and incidents portrayed herein are fictitious. Any similarity to a name, character or history of any actual person, living or dead, is entirely coincidental. All rights reserved. No part of this publication may be reproduced without prior written permission of the publisher.

Note that Australian English is used for this book, as it is set in that country. Spellings will be different to standard spellings used in the United States.

Copyright © 2025 Rowena Wylde
ISBN: 978-1-7640472-2-7

Cover Design: Winsome Books
Image: Depositphotos

eBook Published by Winsome Books 2025
Print Book Published 2026

Adelaide, South Australia

A catalogue record for this book is available from the
National Library of Australia

Also by Rowena Wylde

Ambition and Passion

Maison Angelique

Plan B: Secret Donor Baby

Dangerous Liaisons

Fallen Angel

Avenging Angel

Tainted Angel

Chapter 1

THE VILLA'S MASTER bedroom opened onto a private terrace that seemed to hover above the ocean, and for the first time in eighteen months, Allegra Castelli could breathe. She stood at the glass doors, still clutching her passport and boarding passes, watching the late afternoon sun paint the water in shades of amber and gold. The humid Balinese air wrapped around her like silk after London's perpetual grey chill.

Her luggage lay scattered across the tiled floor where she'd dropped it, too exhausted from the journey to care about her usual methodical unpacking routine. The MBA was finished. The networking events, the case studies, the sleepless nights fuelled by espresso and ambition—all of it belonged to another life now. In five days, she would return to Sydney and whatever came next but for now, she had this: paradise, solitude, and the luxury of no schedule at all.

She retrieved a cold Bintang from the villa's welcome basket and stepped onto the terrace. The beer was crisp against her throat, a small rebellion against the champagne celebrations she'd endured in London. Her father would have laughed at that—Gianni Castelli had raised her on the principle that life's simplest pleasures were often its greatest.

***

The sound of water breaking drew her attention to the adjoining villa. A woman emerged from the infinity pool in one fluid motion, water cascading from her body as she pulled herself onto the pool's edge. Allegra's beer bottle froze halfway to her lips. The woman wore a sleek black one-piece that hugged her athletic frame like a second skin, and she moved with the kind of unconscious grace that made everyone around her seem clumsy by comparison.

Look away, Allegra's rational mind commanded, but her body had different ideas. She took an involuntary step forward, her grip tightening on the terrace railing.

The woman's dark hair was slicked back, revealing sharp cheekbones and a strong jawline that belonged in the pages of *Vogue*. Her skin gleamed bronze in the golden light, and there was something predatory in the way she moved—unhurried, completely in command of her space. She reached for a towel draped over a nearby chair, then paused.

Slowly, deliberately, she turned toward Allegra's villa. Their eyes met across the tropical garden that separated them. The woman's gaze was pale green, almost arctic in intensity, and Allegra felt exposed under that stare—as if every thought in her head had suddenly become visible. Heat rose in her cheeks, but she couldn't look away. The connection was magnetic.

Dangerous Liaisons

The woman's lips curved into the ghost of a smile. She gave the slightest nod of acknowledgment, wrapped the towel around her waist, and disappeared into her villa without breaking stride.

Allegra remained frozen on the terrace, her heart hammering against her ribs. The ocean breeze carried the scent of frangipani and something else—something that made her feel reckless in a way she'd never experienced. She tried to analyse the emotion and categorize it the way she'd been trained to dissect business problems, but it slipped through her mental fingers like water. When had she become someone who became mesmerized by strangers?

The question followed her through her first restless night in paradise, where she lay listening to the waves and replaying those few seconds of connection. By morning, she'd convinced herself it was jet lag, the disorientation of being completely alone for the first time in years. But when she stepped onto Seminyak Beach for her sunrise walk, coffee in hand, she found herself scanning the shoreline with an anticipation that had nothing to do with caffeine.

The woman appeared like a mirage, jogging toward her along the water's edge. She wore black running gear that emphasized every line of her athletic build, moving with the focused breathing of someone who treated fitness like warfare. As she approached, she slowed from a run to an easy jog, then to a walk.

"Mind if I join you?" The voice was lower than Allegra had expected, with an accent she couldn't quite place—

somewhere between Australian confidence and European sophistication.

"Please." The word escaped before Allegra could second-guess herself.

They walked in comfortable silence initially, the only sounds the gentle crash of waves and the distant call of seabirds.

"Beautiful sunrise," the woman said eventually, nodding toward the horizon where the sun painted the sky in brilliant oranges and pinks.

"It's incredible. Such a contrast to London."

"London?" There was genuine interest in the question, not just polite conversation.

"I've been there for my studies. Just finished." Allegra took a sip of her coffee, wondering why she was volunteering information to a complete stranger. "This is my decompression before I go back to reality."

"And where's reality?"

"Sydney. You?"

The woman's smile was enigmatic. "Wherever I happen to be at the moment."

It was a non-answer delivered with such confidence that it felt like a complete response. Allegra found herself intrigued rather than annoyed by the deflection. There was something magnetic about someone so comfortable with mystery.

"What about you?" Allegra asked. "Are you here long?"

"A few days." The woman glanced at her, those pale green eyes assessing. "Just long enough to remember what paradise feels like before returning to the real world."

Dangerous Liaisons

They'd reached the end of the beach where a rocky outcropping marked the boundary of the resort property. The women turned naturally, and began walking back toward their villas. The morning sun had risen during their walk, warming the sand beneath their feet and turning the ocean into a sheet of surging sapphire.

"Thank you for the company," the woman said as they approached the path that led up to their separate accommodations. "I'm not usually one for small talk, but this was... pleasant."

"I'm Allegra."

"I know." At Allegra's surprised look, the woman's smile became more genuine. "Villa registrations aren't exactly state secrets. I'm Meghan."

The name suited her perfectly—in control, strong, with an edge that suggested stories Allegra suddenly wanted to hear. "Meghan," she repeated, testing the sound.

Meghan paused at the fork in the path where their ways would diverge. "Have you eaten? There's a place I know— local spot, not a tourist trap. Unless you're the type who needs to plan every meal in advance."

The gentle challenge in her voice made Allegra's pulse quicken. "I'm trying to be less of that type."

"Good. Twenty minutes?" Meghan's pale green eyes held Allegra's gaze. "I'll pick you up."

Meghan nodded once to confirm her intention, and headed toward her villa, moving with that same fluid confidence that had caught Allegra's attention the day before. Allegra watched her go, noting the way Meghan's posture remained alert even in casual conversation, as if she was always prepared for something—though what, Allegra couldn't begin to guess.

Twenty-three minutes later, Allegra found herself seated across from Meghan at a bamboo table overlooking rice terraces she hadn't even known existed so close to the built up area. The restaurant was tucked away down a narrow path that only locals seemed to know, filled with the aromatic steam of nasi goreng and the gentle chatter of Indonesian families sharing breakfast.

"How did you find this place?" Allegra asked, watching Meghan navigate the Indonesian menu with familiar ease.

"I make it my business to know the real heart of wherever I am." Meghan ordered for both of them in what sounded like fluent Bahasa, her attention completely focused on the elderly woman taking their order. When their food arrived, Allegra discovered she was hungrier than she'd realized. They started with a bowl of tropical fruit, followed by the more traditional food. The simple rice dish was perfectly spiced, nothing like the elaborate presentations she'd grown accustomed to in London's business lunches.

"Better than room service?" Meghan asked, and Allegra caught the hint of smugness in her tone.

"Much better. Though I suspect you knew that."

"I had a feeling you might appreciate authenticity over convenience." Meghan's fingers brushed against Allegra's as she reached for the chili sauce—a contact so brief it might have been accidental—except for the way her eyes lingered on Allegra's face afterward.

They talked easily as they ate, Meghan asking thoughtful questions about Allegra's studies, her plans for Sydney, her family. When Allegra mentioned her father's business, Meghan's interest sharpened.

" Family business?"

" My father started with nothing when he arrived in Australia, but he's worked hard and developed networks in the local community. Import, export—that sort of thing. I haven't been closely involved. He has some development projects in the pipeline. I'm sure I'll hear more about it when I arrive home." Allegra felt the familiar pride that came with talking about her family. "What about you? Family business?"

For just a moment, something flickered across Meghan's features—too quick to interpret, but unmistakably there. "You could say that."

Another non-answer, but delivered with less ease this time. Allegra decided not to push.

After breakfast, Meghan suggested a ride to see the real Bali—not the beaches and resorts, but the temples and villages that most tourists never discovered. She appeared with a motorcycle, sleek and black like everything else about her, and handed Allegra a helmet.

"Trust me?" Meghan asked, and something in her voice made the question feel like more than transportation logistics.

Allegra climbed on behind her, acutely aware of how her body pressed against Meghan's back, how her arms circled Meghan's waist. The motorcycle rumbled to life beneath them, and suddenly they were flying through narrow streets lined with offerings of flowers and incense, past ancient temples and emerald rice terraces that stretched toward volcanic mountains.

At every stop, Meghan was the perfect guide—knowledgeable without being lecturing, respectful of the local customs, somehow always knowing exactly when to speak and when to let the beauty speak for itself. But it was the small moments that made Allegra's breath catch: Meghan's hand on her lower back as she helped her navigate uneven temple steps, the way their shoulders brushed as they stood side by side admiring a stunning view, how Meghan's fingers lingered when she adjusted Allegra's hair after they removed their helmets.

By the time they returned to the villas in late afternoon, Allegra felt as though she'd lived a week in a single day. Her skin was warm from sun and wind, her hair wild from the ride, and she was more relaxed than she'd been in months.

"Pool?" Meghan suggested as they parked. "The day's still warm enough."

Allegra nodded, surprised by how natural it felt to extend their time together. In her villa, she changed into a simple blue bikini, then caught sight of herself in the mirror. Her cheeks were flushed, her eyes bright with something she recognized but had never felt quite this intensely. This would be a holiday to remember. She took a steadying breath and walked to the pool area.

Meghan was already in the water, having changed into that same black one-piece that had first caught Allegra's attention. She swam laps with mechanical precision, each stroke cutting through the water like a blade. Allegra slipped

Dangerous Liaisons

into the pool quietly, not wanting to interrupt the meditation of Meghan's swimming. She completed a few laps to one side of the pool.

When Meghan finally surfaced at the pool's edge near where Allegra floated, water droplets caught the late afternoon light on her skin.

"Better than the gym," Meghan said, slightly breathless.

"Do you always swim like you're training for something?"

"Old habits." Meghan moved closer, close enough that Allegra could see the flecks of blue in her green eyes. "What about you? You move like a swimmer."

"Used to compete in school. These days it's more about clearing my head than winning races."

"And what needs clearing?"

The question was asked softly, intimately, and Allegra found herself being honest in a way she hadn't expected. "Everything. The pressure, the expectations, the feeling like I've been living someone else's idea of success. What's going to happen once I return home." She gave a deprecating laugh. "Nothing major."

Meghan was close enough now that Allegra could feel the current from her gentle treading. "And what does your idea of success look like?"

"You'd think I'd know after the recent studies, but I'm still figuring that out."

"Maybe that's the point of paradise. Finding out what you actually want when no one's watching."

Their legs brushed underwater as they floated facing each other, and neither pulled away. The sun edged lower in the sky, painting the horizon in brilliant oranges and purples, but Allegra was only aware of Meghan's presence, the way the fading light caught in her wet hair, how her proximity made the warm water feel electric against Allegra's skin.

"We should get out," Meghan said eventually, her voice slightly rougher than before. "I'll get your towel."

Allegra pulled herself up the pool ladder, hyperaware of Meghan's eyes on her. When she turned, Meghan was behind her with a plush towel, holding it open. Instead of simply handing it over, Meghan wrapped it around Allegra's shoulders, her hands lingering on the terry cloth, her body close enough that Allegra could smell her sunscreen and something darker, more intoxicating.

"Thank you," Allegra managed, looking up into those pale green eyes before dropping her own, shielding the emotion they surely projected.

For a moment, they stood frozen like that, the air between them charged with possibility. Then Meghan stepped back, the spell broken but not forgotten.

"I should let you rest," Meghan said, though her tone suggested it was the last thing she wanted to do. "Today was..."

"Perfect," Allegra finished.

Meghan's smile was different this time—less controlled, more genuine. "There's a place tonight. Local music, good drinks, not too many tourists. If you're interested in seeing what Bali looks like after dark."

"What time?"

"Nine, if that's not too late? I'll come get you."

Dangerous Liaisons

As Meghan walked back toward her villa, Allegra clutched the towel around herself and watched until she disappeared. The day had been perfect, but she had the distinct feeling that the evening would be something else entirely. Whatever happened, she would make the most of it.

Chapter 2

ALLEGRA STOOD BEFORE her bathroom mirror at eight-thirty, trying to decide if the flowing coral silk dress was too much or not enough. The fabric skimmed her curves without clinging, the colour bringing out the golden highlights in her dark hair and the warmth in her olive skin. She'd let her hair fall in loose waves around her shoulders instead of her usual controlled style—a small act of rebellion that felt significant.

Her hands trembled slightly as she applied a final coat of lipstick. The day had been perfect, but the anticipation thrumming through her body suggested the evening would be something else entirely.

At exactly nine, a soft knock echoed through the villa. Allegra opened the door to find Meghan leaning against the frame, and her breath caught. Gone was the casual daywear; Meghan wore a black dress that was somehow both elegant and dangerous, the fabric cutting close to her athletic frame while leaving just enough to imagination. Her dark hair fell in soft waves, and her pale green eyes seemed to glow in the porch light.

"You look beautiful," Meghan said, her voice lower than usual.

"So do you." The words escaped before Allegra could filter them, and she felt heat rise in her cheeks.

Meghan's smile was knowing. "Ready for Balinese nightlife?"

Rather than take the motorbike, Meghan had ordered a taxi. She explained that they weren't dressed for the bike, plus she could happily drink if they weren't coming home on the bike. The venue was tucked away in a narrow alley lined with local warungs and small shops—nothing like the polished beach clubs Allegra had expected. But when they stepped inside, she understood why Meghan had chosen it. The space was intimate and atmospheric, with low lighting from paper lanterns and the soft sound of gamelan music mixing with contemporary beats. Most of the patrons were Indonesian, with only a scattering of foreigners who'd clearly been guided here by locals.

"How do you find these places?" Allegra asked as Meghan led her to a corner table that somehow had perfect views of both the small stage and the entrance.

"I told you—I make it my business to know the heart of wherever I am." Meghan signalled to a server who approached immediately, as if she were a regular. She ordered for both of them in Indonesian, then turned her full attention back to Allegra. "Besides, I wanted somewhere we could actually talk."

"As opposed to the places where we couldn't?"

"As opposed to the places where everyone would be watching us."

The admission hung in the air between them, loaded with implication. Allegra felt her pulse quicken as she met Meghan's gaze across the small table. The distance between them seemed both too much and not nearly enough. Their drinks arrived—something tropical and complex that tasted like passion fruit and possibilities. Meghan raised her glass in a silent toast, and when their glasses touched, her fingers brushed against Allegra's and lingered.

"So, tell me," Meghan said, her voice pitched low enough that Allegra had to lean forward to hear over the music, "what does Allegra Castelli do when she's not conquering London business schools?"

"I swim. I read. I help with my papa's accounts." Allegra took a sip of her drink, the alcohol warming her from the inside. "I was a very serious child, apparently. Papa used to worry I'd forgotten how to play."

"And did you? Forget how to play?"

Allegra considered the question, aware of how close they were leaning across the table, how Meghan's attention made her feel like the only person in the room. "Maybe. I got so focused on achieving, on making everyone proud, that I stopped asking what made me happy."

"What makes you happy?"

The question was asked with such genuine interest that Allegra found herself being more honest than she'd been with anyone in years. "Moments like this, I think when I'm removed from family expectations. Unexpected opportunities." She pondered her thoughts before answering further. "Moments where I'm not planning or analysing or trying to control the outcome."

Meghan's hand moved across the table to cover hers. "Then stop planning."

The touch sent electricity up Allegra's arm. Meghan's thumb traced small circles on her skin, a gesture so intimate it made Allegra's breathing shallow.

"What about you?" Allegra managed. "What makes Meghan happy?"

For a moment, something unguarded flickered across Meghan's features. "I'm still remembering." She shrugged. "Not surprisingly, being out of the clutches of family also has its attractions."

The music shifted to something slower, more sensual, and couples began moving to the small dance floor near the stage. Meghan stood and extended her hand.

"Dance with me."

It wasn't a question, and Allegra didn't treat it like one. She took Meghan's hand and let herself be led to the dance floor, acutely aware of every place their bodies touched as Meghan's arms encircled her waist.

They moved together as if they'd been dancing for years, Meghan leading with confident grace while Allegra found herself following instinctively. The music wrapped around them, but Allegra was only conscious of Meghan's hands on her waist, the way their bodies fit together, how Meghan's breath felt warm against her ear when she leaned close.

"You're full of surprises," Meghan murmured, her lips barely brushing Allegra's ear.

"Am I?"

"Serious MBA student by day, goddess on the dance floor by night."

Allegra pulled back just enough to meet Meghan's eyes. "Which do you prefer?"

"I prefer the woman who's brave enough to be both."

The space between them disappeared entirely as they continued to move together, their bodies finding a rhythm that had nothing to do with the music and everything to do with the tension that had been building all day. Allegra could feel the solid warmth of Meghan's thighs against hers, the strength in the hands that held her, the way Meghan's breathing had grown slightly uneven.

When the song ended, they remained frozen in each other's arms for a heartbeat longer than necessary. Then Meghan stepped back, her pale green eyes dark with something that made Allegra's stomach flutter.

"Another drink?" Meghan asked, but her voice suggested she was thinking of something else entirely.

"Actually," Allegra heard herself say, "would you like to walk on the beach?"

Meghan's smile was slow and knowing. "I thought you'd never ask."

The taxi ride back to their villas was charged with anticipation. They sat closely with thighs touching. Allegra allowed herself to press closer than strictly necessary, savouring the way Meghan's body tensed in response.

Dangerous Liaisons

On arriving at their resort complex, they dropped their bags in Meghan's villa and walked barefoot down to the beach, the sand cool and soft beneath their feet. The moon was nearly full, casting a silver path across the water, and the sound of waves provided a gentle soundtrack to their conversation.

But they weren't really talking anymore. They were walking closer together than the narrow path required, their shoulders brushing, their hands occasionally touching as they gestured. The sexual tension that had been building all day was becoming impossible to ignore.

"Thank you," Allegra said as they reached the water's edge, "for today. For showing me your Bali."

"It's not over yet."

Meghan stopped walking and turned to face her, and suddenly they were standing close enough that Allegra could see the silver moonlight reflected in her pale green eyes. Close enough that she could smell Meghan's perfume mixed with the salt air.

"Allegra." Meghan's voice was rough with want.

"Yes?"

Instead of answering, Meghan reached up to cup Allegra's face, her thumb tracing the line of her cheekbone. The touch was gentle but possessive, and Allegra felt herself melting into it.

"I don't usually..." Meghan began, then stopped, shaking her head.

"Neither do I," Allegra whispered, understanding perfectly.

When Meghan's lips finally met hers, it was with a hunger that had been building all day—through shared glances and casual touches, through the intimacy of motorcycle ride and poolside conversations. Allegra kissed her back with equal intensity, her hands fisting in the silk of Meghan's dress, pulling her closer.

Meghan's hands tangled in Allegra's hair, angling her head to deepen the kiss. She tasted like their tropical drinks and something darker, more intoxicating. When they finally broke apart, both were breathing hard.

"Your villa or mine?" Meghan asked against Allegra's lips.

"Yours," Allegra replied without thinking, then realized why—she wanted to be in Meghan's space, surrounded by her scent, her presence.

Meghan's smile was triumphant as she took Allegra's hand and led her up the beach toward the villas, the cool grains of sand clinging to their feet, their fingers interlaced with an intimacy that made Allegra's heart thunder. Each step up the curved stone path toward Meghan's terrace felt heavier with anticipation. Her defences, once reinforced by years of careful distance, were collapsing one by one.

Things might be different in the morning, but that was the morning's problem. Right now, there was only the searing heat in Meghan's gaze and the silent promise of a night neither of them would forget.

Meghan's villa mirrored Allegra's in architecture but was entirely different in soul—everything softer, warmer, infused with sensual intent. Candles flickered along the terrace, casting golden light across polished surfaces and woven

Dangerous Liaisons

textures. Either it was all a seduction, or Meghan simply moved through the world like this—surrounded by deliberate beauty.

"Wine?" Meghan asked, voice low, her eyes never leaving Allegra's mouth.

"Later," Allegra murmured, surprising herself with the raw desire in her tone.

Meghan's answering smile was slow and hungry. "Later," she echoed, but she was already moving forward.

Their lips crashed together in the living room, no more pretence or patience. Meghan's hands slid into Allegra's hair, angling her head for a deeper kiss, all fire and control. Allegra moaned into her mouth as their bodies pressed flush, hands wandering, greedy now.

Meghan backed her toward the wall, her thigh slipping between Allegra's, pressing up. "You've been driving me mad all day," she growled against her throat. "The way you talk. The way you look at me like you want to be devoured but don't dare ask."

Allegra whimpered as Meghan's tongue teased the hollow of her neck. "I'm asking now."

Meghan froze for a heartbeat, pulling back just enough to search her face. "You're sure?"

"I've never been surer of anything," Allegra said, voice unsteady but resolute.

Something flickered in Meghan's eyes—hunger tempered by something softer, more dangerous. Emotion. Then it was gone, eclipsed by the searing intensity that returned tenfold.

"Come with me."

She took Allegra's hand again and led her to the bedroom, dark and glowing silver from the moonlight streaming through glass. The bed was wide and low; the sheets rumpled like someone had already dreamed of this moment.

Meghan's hands were slower now, reverent. She slid the straps of Allegra's dress down her shoulders, her lips following the exposed skin with deliberate care. Allegra's breath caught as the fabric pooled at her feet and she stood there, bare and open beneath Meghan's gaze.

"You're fucking perfect," Meghan said, eyes devouring her, hands framing her waist. "Do you know what it does to me, seeing you like this?"

She guided Allegra back onto the bed, then followed her down, their skin meeting, soft and electric. Allegra arched into her touch, her hands roaming over Meghan's back, nails dragging lightly along muscle and spine. Meghan kissed her with a hungry reverence, then lower, tasting the slope of her throat, the soft curve of her breast, teasing with tongue and teeth until Allegra writhed beneath her.

Meghan moved down her body, her hands spreading Allegra's thighs, breath warm against flushed, trembling skin.

"Meghan—" Allegra gasped, fingers tangling in the sheets.

"I want to hear you," Meghan said, her voice low and dangerous. "All of it. Every sound you make when you fall apart for me."

Her mouth found her then, and Allegra nearly sobbed from the shock of it—how precise Meghan was, how slow and devastating. Her tongue worked her in steady, torturous rhythm, flicking, circling, drawing her closer to the edge until her hips bucked and she cried out, fingers fisting in Meghan's hair.

Allegra shattered with a cry, her whole body shaking. But Meghan didn't stop. She pulled her down again—over the edge, again—and only when Allegra was gasping for breath, spent and trembling, did she crawl up and kiss her, deep and slow, letting her taste herself on her lover's lips.

But Allegra wasn't done.

She rolled Meghan onto her back, straddling her hips, her fingers working quickly at the buttons of Meghan's shirt. "You think I'll just lie back and let you have all the fun?" she whispered, her voice low and sultry. "I want to taste *you* now."

She kissed down Meghan's chest, her mouth closing around each nipple in turn, sucking until Meghan arched and cursed softly. Allegra smiled against her skin, then kept going—her mouth, her hands, her whole body intent on unravelling Meghan the way she'd just been unravelled.

And she succeeded. Meghan came hard, with Allegra's name on her lips and her legs trembling, breath ragged. She grabbed at Allegra's hand as the aftershocks rolled through her.

They lay tangled in the sheets, slick with sweat and still catching their breath. Outside, the ocean whispered through the open windows, the scent of salt and candle wax mixing in the air.

"That was…" Allegra began, breathless.

"Yeah," Meghan said softly, brushing hair from Allegra's forehead, pressing a kiss there. "It *was*."

Allegra nestled into her shoulder, too exhausted to speak. Her body was sated, but her heart was still racing. When she woke just before dawn, Meghan was already watching her, her expression unreadable in the dim light.

"Regrets?" Meghan asked.

"None," Allegra replied without hesitation. "You?"

"None," Meghan echoed—but something in her eyes hinted at a future neither of them could predict.

***

The following day began with breakfast on Meghan's terrace, both women moving carefully around the new intimacy between them. The awkwardness dissolved quickly when Meghan suggested exploring local art markets. They spent the day wandering through galleries and workshops, Meghan's knowledge of local artists revealing yet another layer of her mysterious expertise. When a traditional dance performance moved Allegra to tears, Meghan squeezed her hand and whispered explanations of the ancient stories being told. That night, they made love with less urgency but deeper connection, learning each other's bodies with careful attention.

Day Three brought adventure in the form of a sunrise hike up an active volcano. Meghan pushed the pace, challenging Allegra to keep up, and they reached the summit as the sun painted the sky in brilliant colours. At the peak, surrounded by otherworldly landscape, Meghan pulled Allegra into a kiss that tasted like triumph and something deeper. "I've never shared this with anyone," Meghan admitted, and Allegra understood

Dangerous Liaisons

she meant more than just the view. They descended hand-in-hand, stopping at hidden hot springs where they soaked away their exhaustion and made love in the mineral-rich water under a canopy of tropical stars.

Day Four was quieter, more domestic. They cooked together in Meghan's kitchen, with Meghan teaching Allegra to prepare traditional Indonesian dishes while deflecting questions about where she'd learned such skills. "I pick things up quickly," was all she'd say, but the way she moved around the kitchen suggested years of practice. They spent the afternoon reading by the pool, Allegra's head in Meghan's lap as strong fingers played with her hair. When Allegra dozed off, she woke to find Meghan staring out at the ocean with an expression of profound sadness. "What are you thinking about?" Allegra asked. "Tomorrow," Meghan replied simply, and refused to elaborate.

Their final day together carried the weight of ending from the moment they woke. Neither spoke about departure times or travel plans, as if words might make the inevitable more real. They made love with desperate intensity, both trying to memorize every touch, every sound, every sensation. Afterward, they lay in silence until Meghan finally spoke: "We should probably talk about what happens next."

"Do we have to?" Allegra asked, dreading the conversation.

"I think we do."

They dressed and walked to the beach one final time, the setting sun painting everything in shades of gold and goodbye.

Meghan stopped where they'd shared their first kiss, turning to face Allegra with an expression that was carefully controlled.

"This has been..." Meghan began, then stopped, searching for words. "You've given me something I didn't know I needed."

"But?" Allegra prompted, hearing the unspoken limitation.

"But this was paradise. Real life is... complicated. For both of us."

Allegra wanted to argue, to demand phone numbers and promises, but something in Meghan's tone warned her off. "So, this is it? Five days and done?"

"This is perfect exactly as it is," Meghan said firmly. "Some things are meant to be complete in themselves."

"And if I don't want it to be complete?"

Meghan's composure cracked slightly. She looked away, focusing on the horizon in the distance. "Don't make this harder than it has to be."

"I'm not trying to make it hard. I'm trying to understand why it has to end."

"Because I'm not who you think I am," Meghan said quietly. "This has been a simple interlude in our lives."

The cryptic response frustrated Allegra, but she recognized the wall that had suddenly appeared between them. Whatever Meghan was hiding, she wasn't going to share it—not even after five days of intimacy that had felt more real than anything in Allegra's carefully planned life.

"So, what now?" Allegra asked. "We pretend this never happened?"

"We remember it exactly as it was—perfect." Meghan reached out to touch Allegra's face one last time. "Leave it that way. I couldn't bear it if things spiralled downwards away from Bali."

The request felt like a knife to the chest. "Why would you say that?"

"We have lives to lead away from here. I know you'll want to figure this out, make it work somehow. But some things can't be solved."

They walked back to the villas in heavy silence. At the fork in the path, Meghan stopped.

"Thank you," she said simply. "For reminding me what happiness feels like."

"Meghan—"

"Goodbye, Allegra."

Meghan turned and walked away without looking back, leaving Allegra standing alone on the path with her heart breaking and no understanding of why.

Allegra's flight to Sydney departed six hours before Meghan's checkout time, a detail she'd learned from casual conversation on their first day that now felt like a blessing. She couldn't have endured watching Meghan leave.

As her plane lifted off from Denpasar Airport, Allegra pressed her face to the window for one last glimpse of the island that had changed everything. Five days ago, she'd been a woman with a plan—MBA completed, with a new life and opportunities ahead of her. Now she felt like she was leaving half of herself behind in a villa by the sea.

Rowena Wylde

The flight attendant offered champagne to celebrate her journey, but Allegra declined. There was nothing to celebrate about returning to a life that suddenly felt hollow without a mysterious woman who'd refused to let their paradise follow them home.

Chapter 3

THE SYDNEY HEAT enveloped Allegra as she stepped out of the airport, even though she wore a cotton batik dress purchased in Bali. Two years of grey skies and theoretical frameworks hadn't prepared her for the bright Australian sun—or for the familiar weight of expectation that settled on her shoulders the moment she saw her father's car waiting in the pickup zone.

Gianni Castelli hadn't changed. Still the same sharp suit, still the same calculating eyes that missed nothing. He embraced her briefly, perfunctorily, before taking her largest suitcase without ceremony.

"Good flight?" he asked, though his tone suggested he didn't particularly care about the answer.

"Long," Allegra replied, sliding into the passenger seat of his Mercedes. The leather was hot against her back.

They drove in relative silence through the familiar streets of Sydney, past the harbor views that had once taken her breath away but now felt like bars on a cage. It wasn't until they were nearly home that Gianni spoke again.

"Good that you are finally home. Enough of all that theory you've been learning," he said, his hands gripping the steering wheel a little tighter. "Now you learn hands-on about the business. Real business."

Allegra's stomach clenched. She'd known this conversation was coming, had dreaded it through every lecture hall and case study discussion in London. Her father's business practices were not those she wanted to emulate. Ideally, she would find a job elsewhere. "Papa, I thought we could discuss—"

"Discuss what? I've spent a fortune on you over the years. Your education, your living expenses, that fancy degree." His accent thickened slightly, the way it always did when he was agitated. "Now I need some return on that investment."

The word 'investment' hung in the air between them, cold and transactional. Allegra stared out the window at the passing suburbs, each familiar landmark feeling like a step backward from the person she'd been trying to become. Her father always forged a hard deal, and family was no exception.

"There's a big deal coming up," Gianni continued, his voice taking on the tone he used when discussing business— careful, measured, dangerous. "Property development. Could set us up for years if it goes right." He glanced at her sideways. "The people we're meeting with, they operate hotels and casinos. Empire Holdings. Big money, legitimate money."

Allegra's heart stopped. Empire Holdings. She knew of them. Who didn't? They had operations in every state. "When?" she managed to ask.

"Next week. You're coming with me. Look, listen, learn. This is important, Allegra. More important than anything they taught you in those classrooms." His knuckles were white now. "I really need this money."

There was something in his voice she'd never heard before—not quite desperation, but close. It scared her more than his usual commanding certainty.

"What kind of property development?" she asked, though part of her already knew she wouldn't like the answer.

Gianni was quiet for a long moment, navigating through traffic with practiced ease. When he finally spoke, his voice was lower, more careful. "The kind that requires... flexible financing. The tobacco and alcohol imports have been good to us. Very good. But they're also risky. This hotel deal, if it works, it legitimizes everything. Clean money, clean business."

Clean money built on dirty foundations. Allegra closed her eyes, feeling the weight of her MBA—all those ethics courses, all those discussions about corporate responsibility—pressing down on her like a stone.

"They don't know about the... other business?" she asked.

"They don't need to know. Money is money, and ours spends just as well as anyone else's." He pulled into their driveway, the engine ticking as it cooled. "Besides, Franco's handling the construction side. You remember Franco? His boy Riccardo will probably be there too."

The way he said Riccardo's name made Allegra's skin crawl. She'd known Riccardo since they were children, had watched her father's not-so-subtle attempts to push them together over the years. The last thing she needed was another complication.

"Papa, I'm not sure I'm ready for—"

"Ready?" Gianni turned to face her fully for the first time since the airport. "You've had two years to get ready. You've got that fancy degree, all that education I paid for. Now it's time to use it for the family business."

Family business. Such a euphemistic way to describe what was essentially money laundering with a construction front.

"This meeting," she said carefully, "with Empire Holdings. What exactly do you need me to do?"

"Be smart. Be observant. Show them we're not just some family operation run out of a garage." His smile was sharp. "Show them we're sophisticated. Professional. That we understand their world."

If only he knew. The thought of walking into some corporate boardroom, representing her father's questionable business practices to legitimate hotel operators, made Allegra feel physically sick. Her MBA had taught her about corporate ethics and responsible business practices—now she was being asked to be complicit in exactly the opposite.

"I need some time to settle in," she said finally. "To prepare."

"Of course. But Allegra?" Gianni's hand was on the car door handle, but he paused. "This isn't a request. This is family. This is survival. You understand?"

She understood perfectly. She was trapped between the education that had shown her a different way of living and the family that owned her future. Caught between the dreams of legitimate business she'd studied for two years and the reality of what her father expected from her.

"I understand, papa."

But as she followed him toward the house, where the housekeeper waited with arms extended, Allegra realized that understanding and accepting were two very different things. And she had less than a week to figure out which one she could live with.

***

The Empire Holdings boardroom was everything Allegra had expected from a major hotel and casino operation—floor-to-ceiling windows overlooking Sydney Harbour, a polished mahogany table that could seat twenty, and an air of quiet power that seemed to emanate from the very walls. What she hadn't expected was the knot of anxiety in her stomach as she followed her father and Franco through the double doors.

"Gianni, good to see you again," said a silver-haired man in an impeccably tailored suit, extending his hand. "And Franco, always a pleasure."

"Mikhail," her father replied smoothly, his accent carefully modulated. "Thank you for making time for us. This is my daughter, Allegra. Fresh back from London with her MBA."

Allegra stepped forward to shake hands, putting on her most professional smile, when movement at the far end of the table caught her eye. A woman was rising from her chair, turning toward them, and—

Time stopped.

Meghan. The woman from Bali. The woman who had laughed with her over dinner, who had kissed her under the stars, who had whispered against her lips in the darkness. But this wasn't the sensual seductress in sleek black. This was someone else entirely—sharp business suit, hair pulled back severely, an expression of cool professionalism that gave nothing away.

"And this is Mishka," Mikhail was saying, "my daughter. She handles our development acquisitions."

Mishka. Not Meghan. Mishka.

Their eyes met across the polished table, and for a split second, Allegra saw something flicker in those familiar dark eyes—surprise, recognition, something that might have been panic. But then it was gone, replaced by a mask of polite business interest.

"Ms. Castelli," Mishka said, extending her hand with the same cool professionalism she'd shown the men. "Welcome back to Sydney."

Her touch was electric, brief, careful. No one else in the room could have known that these same hands had traced patterns on Allegra's skin just a week ago, that these fingers had tangled in her hair as they kissed in the warm Balinese night.

"Thank you," Allegra managed, her voice steadier than she felt. "It's... good to be back."

They took their seats on opposite sides of the table—literally and figuratively, Allegra realized with growing unease. She tried to focus on the presentations, the

Dangerous Liaisons

architectural plans Franco was spreading across the table, the financial projections her father was discussing with Michael. But her eyes kept drifting to Mishka, who seemed determined to look anywhere but at her.

The meeting started cordially enough, but it didn't take long for the underlying tensions to surface.

"The timeline you're proposing is simply unrealistic," Mishka said, her voice cutting through Franco's explanation of construction phases. "Eighteen months from groundbreaking to opening? For a property of this size and complexity?"

"We've done it before," Franco replied, his jaw tightening slightly. "My crews are the best in the business."

"Your crews may be excellent, but you're not accounting for council approvals, environmental assessments, the inevitable delays that come with waterfront construction." Mishka's tone was professional but firm. "Twenty-four months minimum. More likely thirty."

Gianni leaned forward, his smile tight. "Time is money, Ms. Antonov. Every month of delay costs us both revenues."

"And rushing costs us reputation," Mishka shot back. "Empire Holdings doesn't cut corners."

The temperature in the room dropped several degrees. Allegra watched her father's expression harden—she knew that look, had seen it across dinner tables when business associates pushed too hard.

"Perhaps we should discuss the financial structure," Mikhail interjected diplomatically, but Gianni was already shaking his head.

"The financial structure depends on the timeline. If you're talking thirty months instead of eighteen, we're looking at different numbers entirely. Different arrangements."

"What kind of arrangements?" Mishka's question was sharp, too sharp. Allegra saw her father's eyes narrow.

"The kind that ensure everyone gets what they need when they need it," Gianni replied carefully.

The silence stretched uncomfortably. Allegra could feel the weight of unspoken implications, the careful dance around words that couldn't be said in a room like this. She glanced at Mishka and found her staring back, something unreadable in her expression.

"Perhaps," Allegra found herself saying, "we could take a short break? Revisit the numbers with fresh eyes?"

Mikhail nodded gratefully. "Excellent idea. Fifteen minutes?"

As the men filed out, discussing the harbor views and the weather—anything but the tension that had filled the room—Allegra waited. When the door closed behind them, she was alone with Megan for the first time since Bali.

But Megan was already gathering her papers, not looking up. "I should—"

"The ladies' room," Allegra said quietly. "Down the hall. Two minutes."

Mishka's hands stilled on her documents. For a moment, Allegra thought she might refuse. Then, almost imperceptibly, she nodded.

***

Dangerous Liaisons

The bathroom was mercifully empty, all marble and brass fixtures that spoke of old money and established power. Allegra had barely pushed through the door when she heard footsteps behind her.

"Mishka—"

"Don't." Mishka's voice was sharp, but her composure was cracking. "Not here. Not... God, Allegra, what are you doing here?"

"I could ask you the same thing." Allegra turned to face her, and suddenly they were too close in the confined space, the air between them charged with everything they couldn't say in that boardroom. "Mishka? Really?"

"It's my name. My real name."

"Then who was Meghan?"

Mishka closed her eyes, and when she opened them again, some of the woman Allegra had met in Bali was there—vulnerable, uncertain, real. "Meghan is... when I need to be someone else. Someone who isn't defined by this." She gestured vaguely toward the door, toward the boardroom, toward the weight of expectation that Allegra was beginning to understand all too well.

"Why didn't you tell me who you were?"

"In some situations, I distance myself from the family name. I was there as Meghan, not Mishka. I was free to be..." She trailed off, but Allegra knew what she meant. Free to be herself. Free to kiss a stranger under the stars without it being a business calculation or a family obligation.

"And now?"

"Now we're on opposite sides of a table, representing families that need each other if this deal is to succeed, but apparently don't trust each other very much."

The space between them seemed to shrink. Allegra could smell Mishka's perfume, the same one she'd worn in Bali, could see the pulse beating at the base of her throat.

"Are we?" Allegra asked softly. "On opposite sides?"

Mishka's answer was to close the remaining distance between them, her hands cupping Allegra's face as their lips met in a kiss that was desperate, hungry, full of everything they couldn't say in that sterile boardroom. Allegra's back hit the marble wall as Mishka pressed against her, and for a moment the business meeting, the family obligations, the careful masks they both wore—none of it mattered.

When they broke apart, both breathing hard, Mishka rested her forehead against Allegra's.

"This is insane," she whispered. "My father would kill me if he knew."

"Completely," Allegra agreed, but she didn't step away.

"Your father... the things he was implying about flexible financing..."

"I know." Allegra's stomach clenched. "I'm sorry you had to hear that."

"And my family... we don't just build hotels, Allegra. The casino side of things, it attracts attention. Questions. We can't afford to be associated with anything that isn't completely legitimate."

Dangerous Liaisons

The words hung between them like a wall. Allegra felt the weight of her father's expectations, the dirty money that would fund this deal, the impossible position she'd been placed in.

"We should go back," Mishka said, but neither of them moved.

"Should we?"

Instead of answering, Mishka kissed her again, softer this time, with a tenderness that made Allegra's chest ache.

"This doesn't change anything," Mishka said against her lips.

"No," Allegra agreed, knowing they were both lying. It changed everything.

***

They returned to the boardroom separately, Mishka first, then Allegra two minutes later. The men were already seated, with Mikhail pouring coffee from a silver service while Franco and Gianni maintained careful silence. The tension in the room was palpable, but now Allegra saw it differently—not just business adversaries, but two families trying to find common ground despite their vastly different approaches to commerce.

"Feeling refreshed?" Mikhail asked pleasantly as they took their seats.

"Much better," Allegra replied, avoiding Mishka's eyes but acutely aware of her presence across the table. "Actually, I've been thinking about our timeline discussion."

She could feel her father's sharp attention, Mishka's careful stillness. This was dangerous territory—she was about

37

to speak without his permission, potentially undermine his negotiating position. But her MBA hadn't just taught her about ethics; it had taught her about finding solutions that served everyone's interests.

"What if we approached this as a phased development?" she continued, her voice gaining confidence. "Rather than treating it as one massive project with an impossible timeline, we structure it as complementary phases that can open sequentially."

Franco frowned. "Meaning what, exactly?"

Allegra reached for the architectural plans, spreading them across the table. As she leaned forward, she caught Mishka's eye for just a moment—a flash of curiosity, maybe approval.

"Phase one: the hotel proper. Smaller footprint, eighteen-month completion is realistic. This gives Empire Holdings revenue stream while phase two—the conference facilities and premium suites—is under construction. Phase three would be the retail and entertainment complex."

"That's still the same total timeline," Gianni said, but his tone was thoughtful rather than dismissive.

"Yes, but the revenue starts flowing much earlier. And"—Allegra looked directly at Mishka now—"it allows for proper due diligence on each phase. Environmental assessments, council approvals, all the regulatory requirements that ensure quality construction."

She saw something shift in Mishka's expression. Not just the businesswoman now, but the woman who had talked passionately about sustainable tourism in Bali.

Dangerous Liaisons

"The phased approach also," Mishka said slowly, "allows for adjustments based on market response. If the hotel performs better than projected, we can fast-track phase two. If there are unforeseen challenges..."

"We adapt without jeopardizing the entire project," Mikhail finished, nodding appreciatively. "Clever."

Franco studied the plans with new interest. "Phased construction actually works better for my crews. Don't have to coordinate as many trades simultaneously. Could probably come in under budget on each phase."

"And the financing?" Gianni's question was pointed, but Allegra was ready for it.

"Smaller initial capital requirement. Lower risk for everyone." She glanced at her father, hoping he would understand what she wasn't saying directly. "Phase one financing can be... straightforward. Traditional construction loan against projected hotel revenue. Phase two and three can be financed through the profits from phase one."

The brilliance of it was that it solved everyone's problem. Empire Holdings got their quality assurance and manageable risk. Franco got realistic construction timelines. And her father... her father got a way to legitimize his money gradually, mixing clean revenue from the hotel operation with whatever funding sources he preferred to keep private.

"What about returns?" Mikhail asked. "Our investors expect a certain timeline for full profitability."

"Phase one profitability within two years," Allegra said confidently, "though your operations will be responsible for that. Full development completion and maximum return within five years. But with steady revenue streams throughout, not just a big payoff at the end."

She could see the men doing calculations in their heads, weighing risks and returns. But it was Mishka's reaction she was watching for. Mishka, who understood both the legitimate business concerns and the unspoken complexities of their family situations.

"It's a sound structure," Mishka said finally. "Conservative enough to satisfy our risk assessment, ambitious enough to meet our growth targets. And it provides natural break points if we need to... reassess any aspect of the partnership."

The last part was said with careful emphasis. Allegra understood: if anything about her father's financing became problematic, Empire Holdings could exit cleanly after phase one without being tied to a massive incomplete project.

"Franco?" Gianni looked to his old friend. "Can your people deliver phase one in eighteen months?"

"Hotel and basic amenities? Absolutely. Might even come in at sixteen months if the weather cooperates."

Mikhail nodded slowly. "I have to admit, this addresses most of our concerns. Mishka, what's your assessment?"

Mishka's eyes met Allegra's across the table. For a moment, there was something there that had nothing to do with construction timelines or profit margins—a recognition of the impossible position they were both in, and maybe, just maybe, a way to navigate it together.

"I think," Mishka said carefully, "that Ms. Castelli has found a solution that serves everyone's interests. I'd

Dangerous Liaisons

recommend we move forward with detailed planning for phase one."

Gianni smiled for the first time since the meeting began—not his careful business smile, but something approaching genuine pleasure. "Then we have a deal?"

"We have a framework for a deal," Mikhail corrected diplomatically. "Contingent on the usual due diligence, of course."

"Of course," Gianni agreed smoothly.

As the men shook hands and began discussing next steps, Allegra felt a complex mix of triumph and unease. She'd found a solution, possibly saved her father's deal, and maybe even carved out a space where she and Mishka could navigate their impossible situation. But she was also deeper into her family's business than she'd ever intended to be, complicit in ways her tutors would definitely not approve of.

When the meeting finally concluded and they were gathering their papers, Mishka appeared at her elbow.

"That was well done," she said quietly, her voice pitched for Allegra's ears only. "Very well done."

"Thank you."

"I meant what I said in there. About reassessing if needed." Mishka's eyes were serious. "But I hope we won't need to."

"So do I."

As they walked toward the elevator, Allegra realized that she'd done more than solve a business problem. She'd bought them time—time to figure out how to be on the same side of the table, even when their families weren't. Time to discover whether what had started in Bali could survive the complicated reality of Sydney.

Whether that time would be enough remained to be seen.

Chapter 4

THE EMPIRE HOTEL'S signature restaurant commanded a stunning view of Sydney Harbour, its floor-to-ceiling windows offering a panoramic vista that justified the astronomical prices on the menu. Allegra had to admit her father had chosen well—if you were going to stage a dinner with ulterior motives, you might as well do it somewhere impressive.

"This place has really come up in the world," Franco said, adjusting his tie as they were led to their table. Despite his success, he still carried himself like a man more comfortable on construction sites than in five-star restaurants. "Remember when we first got here, Gianni? We couldn't have afforded a coffee in a place like this."

"Different times, old friend," Gianni replied, but his smile was warm with genuine affection. "We've both done well for ourselves."

Allegra watched the interaction between the two men, seeing echoes of the young immigrants they'd once been. Her father rarely spoke about those early days, but she knew the story—two young men from the same village, arriving in Australia with nothing but ambition and willingness to work harder than anyone else. Franco had gone legitimate, building a construction empire through sweat and determination. Her father... had chosen different methods.

"Allegra, you remember Riccardo?" Franco's voice pulled her from her thoughts.

Riccardo Rossini stood as they approached the table, and Allegra suppressed a sigh. He'd grown into a handsome man—tall, broad-shouldered, with his father's dark eyes and an easy smile that had probably charmed plenty of women. The problem wasn't Riccardo himself, but the transparently obvious way both fathers were watching their interaction.

"Riccardo," she said, accepting his kiss on both cheeks. "You look well."

"And you look stunning," he replied, holding her chair. "London was good to you."

The conversation over dinner was pleasant enough—Riccardo asking about her MBA, sharing stories about the construction business, showing genuine interest in her opinions about the Empire Holdings project. Under different circumstances, Allegra might have found him attractive. He was intelligent, successful, clearly devoted to his father's business. Everything a woman in her position should want. The problem was, she kept thinking about someone else entirely.

"The phased development approach was smart," Riccardo was saying, refilling her wine glass. "Father's been talking about it all week. Says it was the best solution for everyone."

Dangerous Liaisons

"It just made sense," Allegra replied, trying to focus on the conversation. "Sometimes you have to step back and look at the bigger picture."

"Exactly what I told Gianni," Franco interjected. "This girl's got a head for business. Takes after her father."

Gianni's smile was proud, but Allegra caught the calculating look he exchanged with Franco. This wasn't just dinner between old friends—it was an audition. Riccardo was being presented as a suitable partner, someone who could help secure the construction contracts, maybe even provide a legitimate front for less savory activities.

"You know," Riccardo said, leaning closer, "I'd love to show you some of our current projects. Father's got us working on a residential complex in Darling Harbour—cutting-edge design, sustainable materials. Right up your alley, I think."

"That sounds interesting," Allegra replied politely, but her attention was diverted by movement near the restaurant's entrance.

A group of well-dressed diners were being seated at a corner table—clearly VIPs judging by the deference of the staff. And among them, elegant in a black dress that made Allegra's breath catch, was Mishka.

Their eyes met across the restaurant, and Allegra felt that familiar jolt of electricity. Mishka's surprise was quickly masked, but not before Allegra saw the flicker of something that might have been jealousy as she took in the intimate dinner setting, Riccardo's attentive posture.

"Allegra?" Riccardo's voice seemed to come from far away. "You alright?"

"Fine," she said quickly, forcing herself to look away from Mishka's table. "Just admiring the view."

But the damage was done. The rest of the dinner passed in a blur of forced conversation and stolen glances. Allegra found herself acutely aware of how the scene must look to Mishka—herself in an expensive restaurant, being courted by a handsome man while their fathers looked on approvingly. The perfect picture of heteronormative expectations. The thought distressed her. It wasn't just the physical attraction. Now that she had seen Mishka in her business environment, she admired her keen intellect and business acumen. It made her even more attractive.

"I should powder my nose," she said finally, when the tension became unbearable.

"Of course, cara mia," Gianni said, standing politely. "We'll order dessert."

The ladies' room was mercifully empty, and Allegra splashed cool water on her wrists, trying to calm her racing pulse. She was being ridiculous—this was just dinner, just family expectations. Riccardo was perfectly nice, and if she was going to be part of her father's business, she needed to understand all the players.

But when she emerged from the restroom, she found Mishka waiting in the corridor.

"Fancy meeting you here," Mishka said, her tone carefully neutral.

"It's your hotel," Allegra replied. "I should have expected to see you."

"Business dinner?"

There was something in Mishka's voice—not quite an accusation, but close. Allegra felt heat rise in her cheeks.

"Family dinner. My father's old friend and his son."

"His son." Mishka's eyes flicked toward the dining room. "The one who can't take his eyes off you."

"Riccardo's just being polite."

"Is he?"

The question hung between them, loaded with implications. Allegra took a step closer, lowering her voice.

" I'm not interested in him and never will be. You know it's not like that. "

"Do I? Because from where I was sitting, it looked very much like a setup. Two fathers, their successful children, an expensive restaurant..." Mishka's composure was cracking slightly. "Very traditional. Very appropriate."

"And very wrong," Allegra said firmly. "You know what happened between us in Bali. You know how I feel."

For a moment, Mishka's mask slipped entirely, and Allegra saw the woman she'd fallen for—vulnerable, wanting, afraid.

"This is impossible," Mishka whispered. "Our families, the business, everything..." She grabbed Allegra's hand. "Let's get out of here."

"What?"

"Just for a few minutes. There's a terrace on the roof—staff access through the service elevator. Meet me there in five minutes."

Allegra stared at her. "That's insane. If someone sees us..."

"Then we'll deal with it. But I can't sit through another minute of watching you from across a room, pretending I don't know what your lips taste like."

Without waiting for an answer, Mishka turned and walked back toward the dining room. Allegra watched, her heart pounding. The suggestion was crazy, but it wasn't just her heart that throbbed. Another part of her remembered the days if passion.

"Everything alright?" Riccardo asked as she returned to the table.

"Perfect," she lied. "Actually, I'm feeling a bit warm. I think I'll step outside for some air."

"I'll come with you," Riccardo offered immediately.

"No, please. Finish your wine. I'll just be a moment."

She could feel her father's eyes on her as she made her way toward the service corridor, but she didn't look back. The service elevator was exactly where Mishka had indicated, and her heart leaped when she saw it was already ascending.

The rooftop terrace was deserted, the city lights spread below them like scattered diamonds. The harbor bridge dominated the skyline; its steel arches illuminated against the night sky. Allegra had barely had time to appreciate the view when she heard footsteps behind her.

"This is crazy," Mishka said, but she was already moving toward her.

"Completely," Allegra agreed, and then Mishka was in her arms, their lips meeting with desperate hunger.

They kissed like drowning women, all pretence abandoned. Mishka's hands tangled in Allegra's hair, pulling her closer, and Allegra could taste wine and lipstick and something that was purely Mishka.

"I've been thinking about you," Mischka whispered against her lips. "Every day since Bali, every moment in that boardroom..."

"I know," Allegra breathed. "Me too."

They were so lost in each other that neither heard the stairwell door open. Neither saw the figure step onto the terrace, pause, then quickly retreat. Neither noticed the soft click of a phone camera, or the satisfied smile on the man's face as he reviewed the photos.

Down in the restaurant, Riccardo was beginning to wonder where Allegra had gone. And in the shadows of the stairwell, one of his employees was deciding exactly how to use the information he'd just acquired.

The game was about to change dramatically.

***

Allegra paused outside the restaurant's entrance, pressing her palms against her cheeks in a futile attempt to cool the flush she knew was blazing there. Her lips still tingled from Mishka's kiss, her body still hummed with the electricity of being pressed against her on that rooftop terrace. The taste of her lingered—wine and desire and something indefinably intoxicating that made Allegra want to turn around, find her again, and damn the consequences.

But she couldn't. Not here, not now, not with three men waiting at a table who represented everything that stood between them.

She took a steadying breath and walked back into the restaurant, hyperaware of every sensation—the whisper of silk against her skin, the slight tremor in her hands, the way her pulse hadn't quite returned to normal. That woman evoked emotion and passion like nobody had before. Every encounter left Allegra feeling simultaneously more alive and more trapped, caught between who she was becoming and who her family expected her to be.

"There you are," Riccardo said, rising as she approached. "I was starting to worry."

"Just needed some air," she replied, hoping her voice sounded steadier than it felt. "The harbour breeze is lovely tonight."

She slid into her chair, acutely conscious of her father's sharp eyes studying her face. Gianni Castelli had built his empire by reading people, by seeing what others tried to hide. The last thing she needed was for him to detect any lingering traces of her encounter with Mishka.

"You do look better," Franco observed kindly. "More colour in your cheeks."

If only he knew what had put it there. Allegra reached for her wine glass, using the movement to avoid her father's gaze. "Much better, thank you."

"Good," Riccardo said, settling back into his chair with obvious relief. "Because I was hoping to circle back to that invitation. The Darling Harbour project I mentioned—I'd

Dangerous Liaisons

really love to show it to you. We're doing some innovative work with sustainable materials, smart building systems. Right up your alley, considering your business background."

Allegra felt the familiar weight of expectation settling around the table like a net. She could see it in Riccardo's eager expression, in Franco's encouraging nod, in the way her father leaned slightly forward. This wasn't just a casual invitation—it was the next move in a carefully orchestrated game.

"That's very thoughtful of you," she began carefully, but Gianni was already nodding with enthusiasm.

"Good suggestion!" he interjected, his voice carrying that particular tone of paternal authority that brooked no argument. "Allegra would be very interested in seeing your work, wouldn't you, cara mia? It's exactly the kind of hands-on learning experience she needs."

The trap closed with the soft click of inevitability. Allegra found herself nodding, her professional smile feeling like a mask. "Of course. It sounds very interesting."

"Excellent!" Riccardo's face lit up with genuine pleasure. "How about Thursday afternoon? I can pick you up, we'll tour the site, maybe grab lunch afterward to discuss what you've seen."

Another meal. Another day of playing the role of the interested woman, the potential partner, the good daughter making appropriate connections. Allegra's chest tightened, but she kept her expression pleasant.

"Thursday sounds perfect."

"Wonderful," Franco said, raising his wine glass. "To new partnerships and old friendships."

They toasted, and Allegra sipped her wine while her mind raced. She told herself this was manageable—one tour, one lunch, and then she could begin the delicate process of distancing herself from Riccardo without causing offense. He seemed like a decent man; it wasn't his fault he'd been cast in this particular drama.

But distancing herself from her father's business activities was another issue entirely, one far more complex and dangerous. As the evening continued with talk of construction schedules and profit margins, Allegra realized how deeply she was already entangled. Her solution to the Empire Holdings problem hadn't just saved the deal—it had marked her as someone with business acumen, someone worth keeping close.

The trouble was, her father's networks extended far and wide through Sydney's Italian community. If he chose to spread the word that his daughter was unreliable, ungrateful, or untrustworthy, finding legitimate employment would become nearly impossible. Nobody crossed Gianni Castelli—not openly, not without consequences. His reach included everyone from city councillors to bank executives, from construction unions to high-end restaurants. A whispered word here, a casual comment there, and doors would close before she even approached them.

"You're quiet tonight," Riccardo observed, cutting into her thoughts. "Still jet-lagged?"

"A little," she lied. "It's been a big adjustment, being back."

Dangerous Liaisons

"I'm sure it has. London must seem like a different world compared to Sydney."

If only he knew. London felt like a lifetime ago—a place where she'd been free to imagine a future based on merit and ambition rather than family loyalty and carefully managed obligations. Where she could study ethics and corporate responsibility without the bitter irony of knowing she'd never be allowed to practice them.

"It is different," she agreed. "But Sydney has its charms."

Some of them more dangerous than others, she thought, remembering the feel of Mishka's mouth against hers, the way her body had responded with an intensity that left her breathless. Whatever was happening between them was reckless, impossible, and absolutely inevitable. She could try to fight it, try to focus on the safe path her father was laying out, but she knew with bone-deep certainty that she was already lost.

"I think you'll enjoy seeing the project," Riccardo continued. "Father's really proud of what we've accomplished. Clean energy, sustainable practices, community engagement—all the things they probably talked about in your MBA program."

"I'm looking forward to it," she said, and meant it more than he could know. Not because she was interested in Riccardo, but because she needed to understand all the players in this game. If she was going to find a way out—a way to build something legitimate, something that wouldn't compromise her values or her growing feelings for Mishka—she needed to know exactly what she was working with.

"Good," Gianni said, signalling for the check. "It's important for Allegra to understand all aspects of our business relationships. The construction side, the development side, the... various partnerships that make everything possible."

The weight of his words settled over the table. Franco nodded knowingly, Riccardo looked pleased at the prospect of expanded cooperation, and Allegra felt the walls of her carefully constructed future closing in a little more.

But as they prepared to leave, as she accepted Riccardo's polite kiss on the cheek and promised to be ready Thursday morning, she caught sight of Mishka's table across the restaurant. Their eyes met for just a moment—long enough for Allegra to see her own longing reflected there, long enough to remember that not all walls were insurmountable. Some were worth tearing down, regardless of the consequences.

Chapter 5

THE TEXT MESSAGE was simple, almost innocuous: *Need to discuss project timeline. Tonight 9pm. Address attached. M.*

Allegra stared at her phone, her pulse quickening. The address was in Paddington—a boutique hotel tucked away in a quiet street, the kind of place that catered to discretion rather than luxury. She deleted the message immediately, then checked her watch. Seven-thirty. Enough time to create a believable alibi and make her way across the city.

"I'm having dinner with Sarah from university," she told her father, poking her head into his study. "She's back from Melbourne for work. We might be late catching up."

Gianni barely looked up from his papers. "Drive carefully, cara mia. The roads are wet tonight."

If only he knew where she was really going. Allegra grabbed her car keys and headed for the garage, trying to ignore the flutter of nervous anticipation in her stomach. This was reckless—more than reckless, it was dangerous. But the memory of Mishka's mouth against hers, the desperate way she'd whispered Allegra's name on that rooftop, made any rational consideration impossible. She couldn't bear not to be close to her again.

The drive through Sydney's rain-slicked streets should have been routine, but Allegra found herself checking her rearview mirror more often than usual. A dark sedan had been behind her since she left her father's house—nothing unusual in evening traffic, but something about it nagged at her. When she turned onto Oxford Street, the car followed. When she took a deliberate detour through Surry Hills, it was still there.

Paranoia, she told herself firmly. The stress of the situation was making her imagine threats that didn't exist. But as she pulled into the hotel's small parking area, she couldn't shake the feeling that she'd been watched, followed, and catalogued. It wouldn't be beyond her father to keep tabs on her movements—he was a man who trusted nothing to chance, who believed information was the most valuable currency of all.

The sedan drove past without stopping, and Allegra allowed herself to breathe again. Just traffic. Just coincidence. The hotel lobby was dimly lit, with dark wood and leather furniture that spoke of old-world discretion. The desk clerk barely glanced at her as she made her way to the elevator, and Allegra was grateful for the studied indifference that expensive privacy could buy.

Room 312. Her hand trembled slightly as she knocked. Mishka opened the door immediately, as if she'd been waiting just inside. She'd changed from her business attire into jeans and a soft cashmere sweater, her hair loose around her shoulders in a way that made Allegra's breath catch. Without

Dangerous Liaisons

the armour of corporate formality, she looked younger, more vulnerable, achingly beautiful.

"You came," Mishka said softly.

"Did you think I wouldn't?"

Instead of answering, Mishka pulled her inside, pressing her back against the closed door as their lips met in a kiss that was hungry, desperate, full of everything they couldn't say in boardrooms and family dinners. Allegra's hands fisted in Mishka's sweater, pulling her closer, needing to feel the solid warmth of her body, to prove that this was real despite all the obstacles between them.

"As I left the office, I told my grandmother I was having dinner with investors from Melbourne," Mishka murmured against her lips.

"I went with university friend catching up," Allegra replied, then gasped as Mishka's mouth found the sensitive spot just below her ear. "Very mundane cover stories for such scandalous behaviour."

"Scandalous?" Mishka pulled back to look at her, eyes dark with desire. "Is that what this is?"

"What would you call it? Two women from rival families, sneaking around, lying to everyone they know..."

"Necessary," Mishka said firmly, then kissed her again with an intensity that made Allegra's knees weak.

They moved deeper into the room, hands urgent and desperate as they shed layers of pretence along with their clothes. Mishka's mouth found the hollow of Allegra's throat, her teeth grazing the sensitive skin there until Allegra arched against her with a soft moan. Every touch was electric, every caress a revelation that left them both breathless and wanting more.

"I've been thinking about this," Mishka whispered against Allegra's collarbone, her hands sliding down to map the curve of her waist, "every night since the restaurant. The way you looked at me across that table..."

"Mishka," Allegra breathed, her fingers tangling in dark hair as Mishka's mouth travelled lower, leaving a trail of fire in its wake. The hotel room ceased to exist; there was only the heat of skin against skin, the intoxicating scent of Mishka's perfume mixed with desire, the way her body responded to every touch like it had been waiting for this moment its entire life.

When Mishka's lips closed around her nipple, Allegra's back arched off the bed, a gasp torn from her throat that sounded like a plea. Mishka's hands were everywhere—stroking, teasing, claiming—until Allegra was trembling with need, her fingers digging into Mishka's shoulders as waves of sensation crashed over her.

"Please," she whispered, not even sure what she was asking for, only knowing that she needed more, needed everything Mishka could give her.

Mishka's answer was to kiss her way down Allegra's body, her tongue drawing patterns that made Allegra's hips buck against the sheets. When she finally settled between Allegra's thighs, the first touch of her mouth was like lightning, sending shockwaves through every nerve ending until Allegra cried out, her hand fisting in the expensive hotel linens.

Dangerous Liaisons

The rhythm Mishka set was torturous, building her up to the edge of release before pulling back, making Allegra writhe and plead until she was mindless with need. When she finally let Allegra fall over that precipice, it was with an intensity that left her gasping Mishka's name like a prayer, like surrender, like the admission of something that went far deeper than physical desire.

But Allegra wasn't content to simply receive. She pulled Mishka up for a kiss that tasted of salt and desire, then rolled them over, revelling in the soft gasp of surprise that escaped Mishka's lips. Now it was her turn to worship, to explore every inch of silken skin, to discover what made Mishka arch beneath her with breathless moans.

Mishka's body was a symphony of responses—the way she shivered when Allegra's teeth found her pulse point, the soft cries that escaped when Allegra's mouth found her breast, the way her hips lifted desperately when Allegra's hand finally slipped between her thighs to find her wet and ready.

"God, Allegra," Mishka gasped, her head thrown back against the pillows as Allegra's fingers moved in slow, deliberate circles that had her trembling. "Don't stop, please don't stop..."

Allegra had no intention of stopping. She wanted to memorize every sound, every tremor, every way Mishka's body responded to her touch. Mishka's cry of pleasure was music to her ears, spurring her on as she brought her to the edge again and again until Mishka was sobbing her name, her body convulsing with release.

Afterward, they lay tangled in expensive hotel sheets, Mishka's head on Allegra's shoulder, their breathing slowly returning to normal. The rain continued outside, creating a cocoon of intimacy in the small room.

"This is impossible," Mishka said quietly, echoing her words from the restaurant.

"But not non-existent," Allegra replied, running her fingers through Mishka's hair. "We'll find a way."

"Will we? Your father's business, my family's reputation... there are so many ways this could destroy everything we've both worked for."

Allegra was quiet for a moment, thinking about the dark sedan, about her father's watchful eyes, about Riccardo's eager invitation and all the expectations that came with it.

"I think we might already be under scrutiny," she said finally. "I had the strangest feeling driving here tonight. Like I was being followed."

Mishka tensed against her. "Followed?"

"Probably nothing. Paranoia. But it wouldn't be beyond my father to keep tabs on me, especially now that I'm involved in the business. And after that night at the restaurant, if anyone saw us..."

"We have to be careful," Mishka said, lifting her head to look at Allegra. "Until we can work out how we might have a future together."

The words hung between them, heavy with possibility and uncertainty. A future together—it seemed both inevitable and impossible, like something that existed in a parallel universe where family loyalty didn't matter, where business partnerships weren't built on foundations of mutual distrust, where two women could love each other without it becoming a weapon in someone else's hands.

"There's something else," Allegra said reluctantly. "Riccardo asked me to tour his construction sites. Thursday morning."

She felt Mishka stiffen. "And?"

"I couldn't get out of it. My father jumped in immediately, said what a wonderful idea it was, how important it was for me to understand all our... partnerships." Allegra's voice was bitter. "It's another audition, another step in whatever plan he has for my future."

"With Riccardo."

"With Riccardo. With the construction business. With a life that looks exactly like what everyone expects and nothing like what I want."

Mishka was quiet for a long moment, her fingers tracing idle patterns on Allegra's chest. "What if instead of fighting it, you faced it head-on?" Mishka sat up, her business mind clearly working even in their intimate cocoon. "What if you were honest with Riccardo? Made it clear you're not interested romantically?"

"You want me to tell him the truth?"

"Not the whole truth—that would be too dangerous. But you could make it clear that you see this as business only. That you're not looking for romance right now, that you're focused on your career." Mishka's fingers traced idle patterns on Allegra's chest. "It might actually earn you more respect in the long run."

Allegra considered this, thinking about Riccardo's eager expression, his father's expectations, her own father's assumptions. "He won't like it. And my father definitely won't like it if Riccardo feels rejected."

"Maybe not initially. But if you handle it professionally, if you make it about your ambitions rather than about him personally..." Mishka shrugged. "Men like Riccardo respect directness in business. He might be disappointed, but he'll understand."

"And if he doesn't?"

"Then you'll deal with that when it happens. But at least you won't be living a lie, won't be leading anyone on." Mishka's voice grew softer. "I can't ask you to string him along just to make things easier for us. It's not fair to him, and it's not who you are."

It was a risk—being honest always was. But Mishka was right; it wasn't who Allegra wanted to be. She'd spent too many years watching her father manipulate people, use their emotions and expectations as tools. She didn't want to become that person, even for love.

"I'll be honest with him," she said finally. "Professional but clear. No romantic interest, business only."

"He might get annoyed."

"Probably. But I'd rather deal with an annoyed Riccardo than compromise who I'm trying to become." Allegra turned to face Mishka fully. "Besides, if we're going to find a way to be together, it has to be built on honesty somewhere, doesn't it?"

Dangerous Liaisons

Mishka leaned down to kiss her again, soft and lingering, full of promise and regret in equal measure. "Besides," she whispered against Allegra's lips, "let Riccardo show you his construction sites. Let him wine and dine you, let him think he's winning. But when the evening's over, when you've played the part they all want you to play... you come back to me."

The possessiveness in her voice sent heat spiralling through Allegra's body. "Is that an order?"

"It's a request. A very passionate, very desperate request from a woman who's falling harder than she ever intended to."

"Good," Allegra murmured, pulling Mishka down for another kiss. "Because I was already lost the moment I saw you in Bali."

They had until morning to pretend the world outside didn't exist, until morning to love each other without consequences. It would have to be enough—for now.

***

The silver Porsche gleamed under the morning sun as Riccardo pulled into the circular driveway. Allegra watched from her bedroom window, her stomach churning with nervous energy. The conversation she needed to have would be delicate—she had to make Riccardo understand without damaging the families' relationship.

Riccardo emerged from the car with practiced confidence, his tailored suit impeccable despite the early hour. He moved around the vehicle with theatrical precision, opening the passenger door with a flourish before looking up at the house expectantly.

"Showtime," Allegra murmured to herself, grabbing her purse and heading downstairs.

"Good morning, bella," Riccardo called out as she approached, his smile wide and charming. "Ready for our grand tour?"

"Good morning, Riccardo." She managed a genuine smile as she slipped into the passenger seat, the leather warm beneath her. "Thank you for arranging this."

As Riccardo settled behind the wheel, he glanced over at her with satisfaction. "I thought we could make a day of it. After we check out the construction sites and the new warehouse district, there's this fantastic little bistro I know. French cuisine, intimate atmosphere—you'll love it."

Allegra's heart sank. A romantic lunch would make this conversation even more awkward. "That sounds lovely, but perhaps we could keep it simple today?"

"Nonsense," Riccardo waved off her suggestion. "My father would be annoyed if I didn't take you. On the company, of course. It's a business expense."

The first stop was a half-constructed office complex on the outskirts of the city. Riccardo led her through the skeletal framework, pointing out features with obvious pride.

"This will house our new financial services division," he explained, gesturing toward what would eventually be the top floor. "We're expanding the family's corporate interests."

Allegra nodded and made the appropriate sounds of interest. "The location is perfect for attracting corporate clients," she offered, though her mind was elsewhere, rehearsing the words she would need to say.

Riccardo, I want to be clear about where I stand...

I value our families' friendship, but I need you to understand...

This isn't about you personally, but I'm not looking for romance right now...

They moved through three more properties—a renovated warehouse that would serve as a distribution centre, a strip of retail spaces that the family was developing, and finally, a luxury apartment complex that was nearly complete.

"Impressive," Allegra said as they stood in the empty penthouse suite, looking out over the city. "Your father must be very pleased with the expansion."

Riccardo moved closer, his hand settling on her arm. "He is. And he's even more pleased about the prospect of uniting our families." His voice dropped to what he clearly thought was a seductive tone. "As am I."

The presumption in his voice made her stomach tighten. She gently stepped away from his touch. "Riccardo, that's actually what I wanted to talk to you about."

"Oh?" His smile widened, as if he expected her to confess her feelings.

She turned to face him, choosing her words carefully. "I want you to know how much I value the connection between our families. The friendship between our fathers means a great deal to me."

"Of course it does," Riccardo said, moving closer again. "And soon it will mean even more."

"That's just it," Allegra said gently. "I need you to understand that while I have tremendous respect for you and your family, I'm not... I'm not interested in pursuing a romantic relationship."

Riccardo's confident smile faltered. He stared at her for a moment, as if he hadn't heard her correctly. "What do you mean?"

"I mean that I hope we can be friends, but nothing more than that." She kept her voice kind but firm. "It's nothing personal, Riccardo. I'm just not ready for that kind of relationship with anyone right now."

The silence stretched between them. Riccardo's expression shifted through several emotions—confusion, disbelief, and finally, wounded pride.

"Not interested?" he repeated, his voice tight. "Allegra, do you understand what you're saying? Do you understand what you're turning down?"

"I understand that you're a successful, attractive man," she said carefully. "Any woman would be fortunate to have your attention. But I'm not looking for romance right now."

Riccardo let out a harsh laugh. "Not looking for romance? With me?" His voice rose slightly. "Do you have any idea how many women would kill to be in your position right now? How many women throw themselves at me every day?"

Allegra felt a flush of irritation at his arrogance, but she kept her voice level. "I'm sure they do. And I'm sure you'll find someone who appreciates what you have to offer."

"What I have to offer?" Riccardo's face was reddening now. "Allegra, I'm a Rossini. I'm set to inherit one of the most powerful operations in the city. I could give you everything—protection, luxury, status. You'd be untouchable as my wife."

"I don't need those things," she replied quietly.

"Everyone needs those things!" Riccardo snapped, then caught himself, running a hand through his hair. "Look, I get it. You're playing hard to get. It's... it's actually kind of refreshing. Most women are too easy."

Allegra shook her head. "I'm not playing anything, Riccardo. I'm being honest with you."

Riccardo studied her face, and she could see him struggling to accept what she was telling him. Finally, he forced his charming smile back into place, though it looked strained around the edges.

"You know what? Fine. I can be patient." He straightened his tie. "You need time to get to know me better. Once you see what kind of man I am, what kind of life I can give you, you'll change your mind."

"Riccardo—"

"No, it's okay," he said, waving off her protest. "I respect that you're not easy. It just means you're worth the chase. I'm a patient man."

***

The drive back was tense, filled with Riccardo's forced conversation about the properties they'd seen and his plans for the future—plans that, despite her protests, still included her. In his mind, they did. When he finally dropped her off at home, he promised to call her soon.

Allegra stood watching him drive down the driveway. The day hadn't gone as he planned, but Riccardo refused to listen to her. This was going to be more complicated than he'd hoped, but she would change her mind. She had to.

***

Riccardo drove straight to one of his family's legitimate businesses—a high-end restaurant where he often conducted private meetings. In the back office, he found Tony Marcelli, one of his most trusted associates, reviewing inventory reports.

"How'd the tour go, boss?" Tony asked, looking up from his paperwork.

Riccardo loosened his tie and poured himself a drink from the bar in the corner. "She's playing hard to get."

"The Castelli girl? Really?" Tony raised an eyebrow. "That's... unexpected."

"Tell me about it." Riccardo took a long sip of his whiskey. "Every other woman in this city would jump at the chance to be with me, and she's acting like I'm some kind of charity case."

Tony wisely said nothing, sensing his boss's wounded ego.

"But she'll come around," Riccardo continued, more to himself than to Tony. "She has to. Do you know what she's worth, Tony? Her mother left her a trust fund that makes our restaurant profits look like pocket change. Add that to her father's income streams, and we're talking about serious money."

"The kind that could really help with the expansion plans," Tony agreed carefully.

Dangerous Liaisons

"Exactly." Riccardo's eyes gleamed. "My father wants this alliance for the political connections, and the message it sends to the city. But I can see the bigger picture. That girl is sitting on a fortune, and she doesn't even realize how valuable she is."

He finished his drink and set the glass down with a sharp click. "She thinks she can just dismiss me? She thinks she's too good for Riccardo Rossini?" He laughed, but there was no humour in it. "She'll learn. They always do."

Tony nodded, though something in his boss's tone made him uneasy. "What's the next move?"

Riccardo straightened his jacket and checked his reflection in the mirror behind the bar. "Patience, Tony. I'm going to court her properly. Flowers, expensive dinners, shows of power and wealth. By the time I'm done, she'll be begging to be Mrs. Riccardo Rossini."

He headed toward the door, then paused. "And once she is, that trust fund becomes community property. Funny how that works, isn't it?"

***

As Riccardo left, Tony couldn't shake the feeling that Allegra Castelli had no idea what she was up against. Riccardo Rossini wasn't used to being told no, and he'd never met a problem he couldn't solve with the right combination of charm, pressure, and patience. The question was: which one would he use first?

He also had his own card to play. He hadn't realised before how much the Castelli woman was worth. He had to plan his next step carefully.

Chapter 6

THAT EVENING, ALLEGRA closed her bedroom door and reached for her phone. She needed to talk to someone who would understand, someone who knew the pressures of family expectations and powerful men who didn't take no for an answer.

Mishka picked up on the second ring. "Hey, you. How was your day with Prince Charming?"

"Awful," Allegra said without preamble, sinking into the chair by her window. "Mishka, I told him I wasn't interested, and he basically acted like I hadn't spoken."

"What do you mean?"

Allegra recounted the day's events—Riccardo's presumptuous behaviour, his wounded pride when she rejected him, and his insistence that she was just playing hard to get. "He kept talking about what he could give me, what I'd be turning down. Like I'm some kind of business acquisition."

"Which, let's be honest, you probably are to him," Mishka said bluntly. "These guys don't think like normal people, Allegra. They see everything in terms of power and profit."

Dangerous Liaisons

"I know, but I thought if I was diplomatic, if I emphasized that it wasn't personal..." Allegra trailed off, frustrated.

"Did you really think Riccardo Rossini would just graciously accept rejection?" Mishka's voice held a note of exasperation. "His ego is bigger than his father's operation."

"So, what do I do? My father has all but demanded that I marry Riccardo. He thinks it's the perfect solution for both families."

"Stand firm," Mishka said fiercely. "You cannot let them railroad you into this. Once you're married to someone like Riccardo, you become their property. Trust me, I know how these families work."

Allegra felt a surge of gratitude for her lover's support. "I'm scared my father won't give me a choice. He sees this as good for business."

"Then make him understand it's bad for you," Mishka replied. "You're not a bargaining chip, no matter what they think."

There was a pause, and when Mishka spoke again, her voice was bitter. "Speaking of family expectations and being treated like property..."

"What happened?"

"Had another 'family meeting' with my grandmother today," Mishka said, her tone sharp with frustration. "About the future of Empire Holdings."

Allegra could hear the anger in her friend's voice. "Let me guess—Nikolai's still the heir apparent?"

"Oh, it's worse than that." Mishka's laugh was harsh. "Baba sat us both down and laid out the succession plan.

Nikolai eventually gets the CEO position when Father steps down, naturally, because he's the male heir. I get to be his 'trusted advisor' and 'invaluable support system.'"

"That's ridiculous," Allegra said hotly. "You're twice the businessperson Nikolai is."

"Tell that to Baba. She kept going on about how there will 'always be a role' for me in the company, how my contributions are 'deeply valued,' but that Nikolai must be the head because tradition demands it." Mishka's voice dripped with sarcasm. "Apparently, having a woman run Empire Holdings would send the wrong message to our... competitors."

Allegra knew that Mishka's frustration ran deeper than simple career ambition. Empire Holdings was one of the most powerful corporations in the country, with tentacles reaching into construction, real estate, shipping, and dozens of other industries. Officially legitimate, but everyone knew they had government officials in their pocket and weren't shy about intimidating opposition. Sophia Volkov and her husband had built the empire from nothing, ruling it with an iron fist for over three decades. On his death, she assumed the mantle, though Mikhail, her son, was current CEO.

"What did Nikolai say?" Allegra asked.

"That's the worst part," Mishka spat. "He just sat there nodding like a bobblehead. 'Yes, Grandmother. Of course, Grandmother. I'll do my best to live up to the family name, Grandmother.' He doesn't even want it! He'd rather be playing golf and collecting vintage cars, but he's too scared of her to say no."

"And you want it."

Dangerous Liaisons

"I don't just want it, Allegra. I'm meant for it. I know every aspect of our operations better than anyone except Baba herself. I've been groomed for leadership my entire life, but apparently, having the wrong chromosome disqualifies me from actually leading."

Allegra could hear Mishka pacing, could picture her friend's usual controlled composure cracking under the weight of her frustration.

"Baba keeps talking about how proud she is of me, how I'm her favourite, how brilliant I am," Mishka continued. "But when it comes to the one thing that matters—the family name and actually inheriting what she's built—suddenly I'm relegated to being Nikolai's assistant."

"Have you talked to her about it? Really talked to her?"

"Oh, I've tried. You know what she says? 'Mishka, darling, you're invaluable to this family. But the world we operate in requires a certain... image. Men respect men. Our associates expect traditional leadership structures. You'll have real power, just not the title.'"

Mishka's voice cracked slightly. "Fifty years of breaking barriers, of proving that a woman can build and run an empire, and she's still bowing to tradition when it comes to succession."

"I'm sorry," Allegra said quietly. "That has to be devastating."

"You know what the really twisted part is? I love her. Baba is my hero. She's the strongest person I've ever known. But she's also the one person standing between me and everything I've worked for."

The parallel between their situations wasn't lost on either of them. Both women were being constrained by the expectations of powerful families, their futures dictated by traditions and business considerations rather than their own desires.

"At least you have a choice," Mishka said after a moment. "You can refuse Riccardo. You can walk away from your father's plans. I can't walk away from being Sophia Volkov's granddaughter."

"I don't know if I really have a choice either," Allegra admitted. "You should have seen Riccardo today. He was so confident that he could change my mind, like my opinion was just an obstacle to overcome. And my father... he's so invested in this alliance."

"Then we both have to fight," Mishka said firmly. "We can't let them decide our lives for us, Allegra. I may be stuck with Nikolai inheriting, but I'm going to make damn sure I have real power, not just a pretty title. And you're going to make sure you don't end up married to someone who sees you as a trust fund with legs."

Allegra smiled despite her anxiety. "When did we become the rebels in our families?"

"The moment we realized we deserved better than what they were offering us," Mishka replied. "Now, what's your next move with Riccardo?"

"I don't know. He's planning to 'court' me properly, as he put it. I think he genuinely believes he can win me over."

"Let him try," Mishka said, her voice turning calculating. "But document everything. Keep records of his behaviour, his

Dangerous Liaisons

words, his presumptions. If this gets ugly—and with men like Riccardo, it usually does—you'll want evidence of what you're dealing with."

"You think it will get ugly?"

"I think Riccardo Rossini isn't used to being told no, and I think your trust fund makes you too valuable for him to just walk away. Be careful, Allegra. These families don't play fair when they want something."

As they hung up, Allegra sighed with the weight of their circumstances. In different ways, they were both fighting against the constraints of powerful families who saw them as pieces on a chess board rather than individuals with their own ambitions and desires. The question was: how far would those families go to get what they wanted?

***

Over the following weeks, the business relationship between Empire Holdings and the Castelli-Rossini consortium moved into formal negotiations. The conference room on the fortieth floor of Empire Holdings became a familiar setting, with teams of lawyers shuffling contracts and representatives from all three families working through the finer points of what would become a multi-billion-dollar partnership. They had settled on the name of *Harbour Light* for the development, given that it's location would be on the shores of the harbour.

Allegra found herself attending these meetings regularly now, with her father still insisting that she needed to understand the family's business dealings. "You'll be part of this world whether you marry into it or inherit it," Franco had told her. "You need to know how these relationships work."

What made the meetings unbearable was Riccardo's constant presence. He'd positioned himself as his father's key representative, and he never missed an opportunity to make pointed remarks about their future together—always in front of the fathers, always with that presumptuous smile that made Allegra's skin crawl.

"As the next generation and with combined interests," he'd say casually while discussing long-term contract provisions, "Allegra and I want to ensure the partnership benefits both our families equally."

Or: "Allegra's going to love the new development on the Gold Coast. We could inspect progress together."

Each comment was calculated to reinforce the assumption that their relationship was inevitable, and Allegra watched her father nod approvingly while Franco beamed with satisfaction. Every time she tried to subtly deflect or change the subject, Riccardo would just smile wider, as if her discomfort was charming.

Across the mahogany conference table, Mishka sat with increasing frustration as the meetings progressed. She'd attended these sessions for years, but now Nikolai was always beside her, introduced as "the future of Empire Holdings" while she was merely "our invaluable family representative."

Allegra watched the subtle dynamics play out with growing anger on her friend's behalf. When complex operational questions arose, the men would automatically turn to Nikolai, who would then glance helplessly at Mishka before offering vague, surface-level responses. Mishka would then step in with detailed knowledge of operations, regulatory requirements, and profit margins, but the credit always seemed to flow back to her brother.

"Nikolai's been working closely with our logistics team," Mikhail would say proudly, even though everyone in the room knew it was Mishka who'd revolutionized their shipping operations.

"Your boy really understands the hospitality industry," Gianni would comment, while Mishka's comprehensive market analysis sat in front of him with her name clearly printed on the cover.

The most infuriating part was Nikolai's passive acceptance of the credit. He never corrected the inaccuracy or acknowledged his sister's contributions. He simply nodded and smiled, comfortable in his inherited authority.

During one particularly tense session about territorial agreements, Riccardo made another of his presumptuous comments: "Allegra's going to be busy managing the social aspects of these partnerships once we're settled. Women have such a natural talent for relationship building, don't they?"

Allegra felt her jaw clench, but before she could respond, her eyes found Mishka's across the table. Her friend's expression was carefully neutral, but Allegra could see the flash of anger in her eyes—not just for the sexist comment, but for the entire situation they both found themselves in.

Mishka gave the slightest shake of her head, a warning not to react, followed by an almost imperceptible nod of understanding. They were both trapped in this room, forced to smile and nod while the men around them made decisions about their lives and futures.

When Mikhail began discussing a previous Volkov development, automatically deferring to Nikolai despite the fact that Mishka had personally overseen the entire project, Allegra caught her friend's eye again. This time, she let her own frustration show—a slight tightening around her eyes, a barely perceptible grimace of sympathy.

Mishka's response was equally subtle: a tiny lift of her chin, a brief flash of determination in her expression. They were both fighting battles they couldn't win openly, but at least they weren't fighting them alone.

As the meeting dragged on, Riccardo grew bolder. When the discussion turned to the new construction project timeline, he moved his chair closer to Allegra and placed his hand on her arm while speaking.

"Allegra and I were just discussing this property during our tour last week," he said, his fingers tightening possessively. "She was very impressed with the potential."

Allegra gently but firmly removed her arm from his grasp. "I thought the location was well-chosen," she said carefully. "Though I have some concerns about the environmental impact assessments."

It was a deflection, but Riccardo's smile faltered slightly at her withdrawal from his touch. She saw something flicker in his eyes—irritation, perhaps, or wounded pride—before the charming mask slipped back into place.

Dangerous Liaisons

"Always thinking about the community impact," he said, his tone just slightly patronizing. "That's what I respect about you."

Across the table, Mishka's knuckles were white where she gripped her pen. When she spoke, her voice was professional but tightly controlled: "Actually, the environmental assessments raise some significant concerns that could affect our timeline. Perhaps we should table this discussion until we have more complete data."

It was a lifeline, and Allegra grabbed it gratefully. "That's an excellent point. We shouldn't proceed without full information."

Franco nodded approvingly. "Cautious and thorough. Don't let it delay progress however. Time is money."

But Allegra noticed that he'd addressed his comment to her, not to Mishka, even though Mishka had initiated the suggestion. Another small reminder of how invisible competent women could be in rooms full of powerful men.

As the meeting finally ended and people began filing out, Allegra managed to catch Mishka's eye one more time. This time, her friend's expression was unmistakably clear: *We need to talk.*

The question was when they'd have the chance to do so without the watchful eyes of their families—and whether they could find a way to support each other through the battles ahead.

Chapter 7

THREE DAYS LATER, Allegra found herself in Mishka's penthouse apartment, the harbour visible through floor-to-ceiling windows. It was one of the few places they could speak freely, away from the scrutiny of their families and the political manoeuvring that followed them everywhere.

Allegra had fallen back on the claim she was having dinner with a friend. Which she was. She just hadn't mentioned who, or why.

"I can't do this anymore," Mishka said without preamble, handing Allegra a glass of wine. "Sitting in those meetings, watching them give Nikolai credit for my work, pretending I'm grateful for whatever scraps of authority they throw my way."

Allegra settled into the plush sofa, noting the tension in her friend's shoulders. "What are you thinking?" She reached out to massage the neck in the area she could reach. Mishka's muscles were tight under her touch, but slowly began to soften in response to the pressure.

"I'm thinking about leaving." Mishka had shut her eyes and exhaled, moaning softly at the pleasurable pain. When she

Dangerous Liaisons

spoke again, her voice was determined. "I want to do it. Start my own company. Build something that's mine."

The statement hung in the air between them. Allegra knew what it meant—the courage it would take, the bridges it would burn.

"Have you told your grandmother?"

Mishka laughed bitterly. "Are you kidding? She'd have me committed. No, this has to be done carefully. Quietly. And I can't do it alone."

She turned to face Allegra directly, her eyes intense. "I want you to join me."

Allegra's heart skipped. "Mishka—"

"Hear me out." Mishka moved closer, her passion evident. "You have an MBA from the London Business School. You understand international business, finance, marketing. You've been watching your father's operations for years. And you're trapped in the same cage I am."

"What kind of business?" Allegra asked, though part of her already knew she was intrigued.

Mishka's eyes lit up. "Boutique hotels. High-end, exclusive. But not just any hotels—places designed specifically for women executives. Professional women who need somewhere safe, sophisticated, discreet."

She moved to her laptop, pulling up files she'd clearly been working on for months. "Look at this. Luxury accommodation, but with 24-hour business centres, private meeting rooms, wellness facilities. Spa services, fitness centres, healthy dining options. Everything designed with the professional woman in mind."

Allegra leaned forward, studying the preliminary designs and market research. "I love the concept. I know so many women who would appreciate something like this."

"I want to create spaces where women like us can conduct business without being hit on by drunk businessmen at the hotel bar. Where we can have confidential meetings without worrying about being overheard or undermined. Where we can actually relax and recharge."

The concept was brilliant. Allegra could see the potential immediately. Her mind whirled as she thought through the possibilities.

"Club atmosphere," Mishka continued, "but for a membership that's actually useful. Networking events, mentorship programs, partnerships with women-owned businesses. We could create a whole ecosystem."

"The startup costs alone would be enormous," Allegra cautioned, though she was already calculating possibilities.

"Which is where you come in." Mishka's smile was hopeful. "Your trust fund. My connections and operational knowledge. Together, we could make this work."

Allegra felt a flutter of excitement at the thought of a permanent working relationship with Mishka, followed immediately by a wave of reality. "My father would challenge me leaving. He'd see it as betrayal—me taking money that should strengthen the family business and using it to develop my own interests. Totally forgetting of course that my mother left that money for me, not for his business."

"Would that be considered disloyal?"

Dangerous Liaisons

"In his mind? Absolutely. Any business venture that isn't directly tied to family interests is seen as disloyalty. And if I'm not married to Riccardo, if I'm not cementing the alliance with the Rossinis..." Allegra trailed off, the implications clear.

Mishka moved closer, her hand finding Allegra's. "Maybe I can position this as an expansion of Empire Holdings' business and that way, my family won't be seen to lose face by my defection, but there shouldn't be any mis-understanding. This has nothing to do with them."

"You're right, but... I think you know a little about family honour. It means so much in a family like mine."

"We do this for ourselves," Mishka said firmly. "Not as an extension of their businesses, not as some subsidiary they can control. This is ours. If I can swing my grandmother on our side, that will make a difference. My father will not dare go against her, and Nikolai might be glad to get me out of the way."

Allegra felt the warmth of Mishka's hand, the intensity of her gaze. There was something intoxicating about being around someone who shared her ambition, who understood the frustration of being sidelined despite her capabilities.

"That means I'll need to figure out how to access my trust fund," Allegra said. "I've never needed to before—everything I've wanted has been provided. But for something like this..."

"Can you access it independently?"

"I honestly don't know. I'll need to meet with the trustees, understand the terms. My mother set it up to protect me, but I'm not sure if that protection extends to protecting me from my own family's disapproval."

Mishka nodded thoughtfully. "I think I can eventually get Grandmother's support. She respects bold business moves, and she and my grandfather built their empire by taking risks others wouldn't. But it will take time to present it right."

"And if she doesn't support it?"

"Then we do it anyway." Mishka's voice was resolute. "I'm tired of waiting for permission to live my life, Allegra. We're both smart, capable women who've been trained by some of the most successful business minds in the country. The only thing holding us back is other people's expectations."

The proximity between them was charged with possibility—not just business possibility, but something deeper. Allegra could feel the pull of Mishka's vision, the allure of finally taking control of her own future.

"I'll investigate the terms of my trust fund access," Allegra said quietly. "And you'd need to decide if you can act outside of your family's operations."

"I've already decided." Mishka's thumb brushed across her knuckles—slow, reassuring, charged. "This could be our chance. Our chance to build something together, something that's ours."

The word together hung between them like a promise, layered with longing and intent. Allegra's pulse quickened as Mishka's hand rose to cup her cheek, her touch feather-light but crackling with electricity.

"I've been thinking about this for months," Mishka whispered, her breath warm against Allegra's lips. "About working with someone who actually gets it. Someone who wants more. Someone who wants me."

Dangerous Liaisons

Their faces were close now—so close—and Allegra could feel the tension stretch between them like a drawn bow. Every unspoken desire, every late-night meeting, every restrained glance—they all culminated in this one, aching moment.

When Mishka kissed her, it was a collision of relief and hunger. Soft at first, coaxing, then deeper as Allegra melted into it with a breathy sigh. The kiss was a revelation—urgent, consuming, edged with the sharpness of everything they'd had to suppress.

Here was someone who didn't see her as a political pawn or a trust fund heiress, but as a woman burning with ambition, intelligence, and desire.

"I want this," Allegra murmured against her lips, her hands threading through Mishka's dark hair, tugging gently to bring her closer. "The business, the partnership... you."

"Even if it means turning everything upside down?"

"Especially then. I've never been surer of anything. You've brought clarity to my life, filling a chasm I'd never realised was there."

Mishka answered with a growl low in her throat, pulling Allegra against her. Their bodies aligned with breathtaking precision, the business plans on the coffee table fluttering to the floor as passion overtook pretence.

"Come with me," Mishka said, her voice rough with want, her hands skimming down Allegra's back, tracing every curve like she'd already memorized it.

They moved through the penthouse, the gleam of city lights turning walls into mirrors and shadows into temptation.

The bedroom was a cocoon of silk and desire, waiting to be undone.

Mishka turned, facing Allegra with a hunger so raw it made her breath catch. There was no hesitation now—just need, honest and wild. She reached for the buttons of Allegra's blouse, her fingers deft but unhurried, undoing each one like unwrapping a secret.

"I've wanted you like this for so long," she whispered, her lips grazing the skin she bared—collarbone, shoulder, the swell of a breast. "Every time I watched you keep your cool when they tried to box you in... I wanted to worship you."

Allegra let out a soft gasp, her body already arching into the contact. Her hands slid under Mishka's blouse, pushing it up and over her head, revealing smooth skin and taut muscle. Their mouths met again, this time hungrier, teeth and tongues and moans shared like confessions.

"You're mine tonight," Mishka murmured, her mouth claiming the delicate curve of Allegra's neck, biting just enough to make her gasp. "All mine."

Clothes fell away in a blur, replaced by heat, skin, breath. They tumbled onto the bed, silk sheets cool beneath them, every touch a promise and a provocation. When Mishka's mouth closed around Allegra's nipple, sucking slowly, deliberately, Allegra cried out, her hips rising instinctively.

"Mishka, God—please..." Her voice was ragged, trembling with need.

"Please what?" Mishka asked, her voice velvet and smoke. "Tell me."

"I want you. I want to feel something real."

Dangerous Liaisons

Mishka's response was a slow, wicked smile—and then her mouth was traveling lower, past the trembling of Allegra's stomach, the quiver in her thighs. When she settled between Allegra's legs and her tongue made contact, Allegra's back arched off the bed, a moan tearing from her throat.

The rhythm was unrelenting and reverent, building her up, drawing her out. Mishka worshipped her with every flick of her tongue, every stroke of her fingers, until Allegra came apart with a cry that shook the walls.

It wasn't just release—it was liberation.

Later, limbs tangled and skin still humming, Allegra traced idle circles across Mishka's bare shoulder.

"I didn't know it could feel like this," she whispered.

"Like what?"

"Like freedom. Like us."

Mishka turned her head, kissed her slow and deep. "This is just the start, Allegra. We're going to build an empire that no one sees coming."

They made love again, slower this time—an exploration instead of a storm, each kiss a blueprint, each caress a foundation. And somewhere in the space between silk sheets and whispered promises, the future began.

***

Several floors below, Tony Marcelli sat in his car reviewing the photographs on his camera. The intimate silhouettes glimpsed fleetingly in the penthouse window told a clear story—one that Riccardo Rossini definitely wouldn't like hearing.

Tony drummed his fingers on the steering wheel, thinking. He'd worked for the Rossini family for fifteen years, long enough to understand the dynamics at play. Riccardo was his boss, technically, but Tony had never been impressed with the younger Rossini's leadership style. The man was arrogant, impulsive, and had a nasty habit of shooting the messenger when he didn't like the news.

This information was explosive. Riccardo's intended bride wasn't just rejecting him—she was actively involved with another woman. And not just any woman, but Mishka Volkov, granddaughter in one of the most powerful business families in the country.

Tony could deliver the photos to Riccardo as ordered, watch his boss lose his temper and probably make some stupid, vengeful decision that would blow up in everyone's faces.

Or...

Tony looked at the photos again, thinking about what he'd observed. Their discussions as they poured over sheets of paper had looked intense. It was amazing what a telephoto lens could pick up. Not enough to read the writing unfortunately. Those two women were planning something big, something that could be very profitable for someone who got in on the ground floor. Someone who had information they needed to keep quiet.

Riccardo saw Allegra Castelli as a walking money pit, a means to an end. But Tony was beginning to think she might be something much more valuable than that—especially if she had Mishka Volkov as a partner.

The question was: would it be more profitable to serve his arrogant boss's wounded pride, or to play a longer, more strategic game?

Tony started the engine, but instead of heading to Riccardo's location, he drove home. He needed time to think about this, to consider all the angles.

Riccardo Rossini might be his boss, but that didn't mean Tony had to be as short-sighted as he was. Sometimes the smart money was on backing the winning horse, even if it wasn't the one that was paying your salary.

Especially when that horse didn't even know it was in a race yet.

Chapter 8

MISHKA HAD CHOSEN the location carefully—a discreet cocktail bar in Darlinghurst, well away from any of the Antonov family hotels. She needed Nikolai on side, and that meant having a conversation without the weight of family expectations pressing down on them. Allegra joined them also, having slipped away from her father's corporate office.

Nikolai entered hesitantly, having no idea why his sister had asked him to join the two women. He greeted Allegra cordially, ordered a drink, then sat down with an expectant look on his face. "Why do I get the feeling you two have something underhand going on? Spill."

"Totally above board as far as I'm concerned, but father and grandmother might not agree." Mishka outlined the details of her plan, including the role she had offered Allegra.

Nikolai turned a bemused look on Allegra. "So, you want to poach my sister and start a rival hospitality business?" He swirled the whiskey in his glass with apparent amusement.

Allegra leaned back in the leather booth, projecting confidence she didn't entirely feel. "There's more to it. It's focusing on a market that Empire Holdings hasn't addressed, and frankly, your company wouldn't do it well. It takes a woman to understand the needs of women. Mishka has vision and talent that's being wasted in middle management. She could run her own operation, make her own decisions."

"And coincidentally, this removes her from the succession conversation at Empire Holdings," Nikolai observed, but his tone wasn't accusatory—if anything, he sounded intrigued.

Allegra and Mishka exchanged a wordless glance. Nikolai had picked up of the part of their proposal that had the most significance for him. "Would that be such a bad thing?" Mishka asked quietly. She'd been letting Allegra lead the conversation, but now she leaned forward. "You know as well as I do that people look to me first, even though you're the heir. It's not fair to either of us."

Nikolai was quiet for a moment, considering. The truth was, he'd felt the weight of those expectations his entire life—the subtle comparisons, the way board members' eyes would drift to Mishka during meetings, the unspoken question of whether bloodline or competence should determine leadership.

"Explain your thinking for this business concept," he said finally.

"Boutique hotels for women," Mishka said. "High-end, personalized service. Think of it as the luxury market that Empire Holdings has never quite cracked."

"Interesting." Nikolai raised his glass in a mock toast. "And here I thought my sister was just trying to bring bright talent into *our* company."

"Your sister has excellent taste in business partners," Allegra laughed, some of the tension easing from her shoulders.

"That she does," Nikolai agreed with a fond look at Mishka.

Out of the corner of her eye, Allegra noticed a dark-suited figure moving with purpose in their direction. Their moment of levity was shattered when Riccardo Rossini appeared at their table like a storm cloud given human form.

"Well, well. What do we have here?" Riccardo's voice cut through the ambient jazz music, drawing unwanted attention from neighbouring tables. He slid uninvited into the booth, forcing Allegra to shift uncomfortably toward the wall.

"Riccardo," Allegra said carefully. "What are you doing here?"

"Funny thing about this city," he replied, his smile sharp as broken glass. "It's smaller than people think. Not much happens in this city that I don't learn about. I thought you knew that."

The implied threat in his words made Mishka's skin crawl. Riccardo's surveillance of Allegra was more extensive than they'd realized, and the way his eyes lingered on her and Mishka together suggested he knew more than he was letting on.

"You still haven't answered my question. What are you doing here?"

"Making sure you're not working on deals that exclude Rossini Constructions. We're in a consortium, remember?"

Dangerous Liaisons

"We're having a private meeting," Nikolai said coolly. "Family business."

"Family business that doesn't include the man who's going to marry into the Castelli family?" Riccardo's laugh was harsh. "That seems short-sighted."

"There's nothing to marry into," Allegra said firmly. "I thought I made that clear."

The temperature at the table dropped several degrees. Riccardo's carefully constructed charm cracked, revealing something uglier underneath.

"Clear? You think you can just dismiss me like some nobody?" His voice rose incrementally with each word, drawing stares from other patrons. "Do you have any idea what you're throwing away?"

"I know exactly what I'm refusing," Allegra shot back, finding strength in Mishka and Nikolai's presence. "A marriage based on business arrangements and family expectations instead of love or respect."

Riccardo's face flushed red. "Love? Respect? Jesus Christ, Allegra, grow up. This isn't some romance novel. This is about family, about honouring commitments, about—"

"About what you can get out of it," Mishka interrupted coldly.

Riccardo turned his attention to her, his eyes narrowing. "I don't recall asking for your opinion, Miss Volkov."

"You didn't ask for mine either," Nikolai said, his voice carrying the quiet authority he'd inherited from his father. "But you're going to get it anyway. It's time you left."

"Actually, I think it's time we all got some clarity," Riccardo said, his voice dropping to a dangerous whisper. "Let me explain something to Allegra about family obligations, about consequences."

He leaned closer to Allegra, and she could smell the whiskey on his breath, see the desperation he hid behind anger.

"Your refusal to honour the expectation of our families isn't just hurting me—it's going to destroy everything our fathers have built together. Gianni Castelli and Franco Rossini have been partners for thirty years. They're pillars of the Italian community in Sydney. If you keep playing these games, I'll make sure my father pulls out of every joint project, every shared investment."

"Riccardo—"

"I'm not finished." His hand slammed on the table, causing drinks to slosh and conversations to halt around them. "The Meridian project alone represents fifty million dollars in development. Your father's company is leveraged to the hilt on that deal. If we pull out, Castelli Enterprises won't just lose money—it'll go under entirely."

The threat hit its target. Allegra's face went pale, and she clenched her hands into fists. Mishka reached out with a supporting hand on her thigh beneath the table. Allegra drew strength from the touch. "You wouldn't destroy a lifelong friendship over this."

"Try me." Riccardo's smile was predatory. "If you don't give me a chance—a real chance—I'll make sure everyone in our community knows how ungrateful you are. How you spat in the face of family tradition and honour. Your family's reputation will be in ruins, and the debt they owe us." He leaned even closer. "My father will add interest and demand immediate payment. Full payment."

The silence that followed was suffocating. Around them, the bar's normal chatter had resumed, but their corner booth felt like the eye of a hurricane. Allegra had the impression that other patrons were no longer looking in their direction, but were doing their best to listen still.

"You're talking about destroying lives over wounded pride," Mishka said quietly, her voice cutting through Riccardo's bluster like a blade.

"I'm talking about honour," Riccardo snapped. "About keeping promises. About understanding that actions have consequences." He stood abruptly, straightening his jacket with sharp, angry movements. "Think about it, Allegra. Think about your father, your family's legacy, everyone who depends on Castelli Enterprises staying solvent. Is your petty rebellion really worth all of that?"

He stormed out without another word, leaving behind a tension so thick it felt hard to breathe. The silence stretched for several minutes after Riccardo's departure. Finally, Nikolai signalled the waitress for another round.

"What a complete piece of shit," he muttered, his usual composure thoroughly shaken.

Allegra stared at her untouched martini, her face pale. "For the record, there may have been an unspoken family expectation, but marriage with Riccardo has not been openly raised. There is no agreement, formal or otherwise. He's not wrong about the debt though," she added quietly. "The

Meridian project... papa's put everything into it. If the Rossinis pull out..."

"That doesn't give Riccardo the right to threaten you," Mishka said firmly. " His reaction is over the top, and it sure as hell doesn't mean you have to marry him to save your family's business. You're not a sacrificial goat."

"Doesn't it?" Allegra's laugh was bitter. "You heard him. Thirty years of partnership, millions of dollars, the entire Italian community watching. If I don't comply, he'll destroy everything my father has worked for."

Mishka leaned across the table, forcing Allegra to meet her eyes. "He's bluffing. What we just saw was a desperate man. There's a motivation behind this. We just need to find it."

"What are you suggesting?"

"I'm suggesting we fight fire with fire." Mishka's smile was sharp as broken glass. "Riccardo wants to play dirty? Let's show him what dirty really looks like."

Nikolai had been quiet, processing what he'd witnessed. Now he leaned forward, his expression thoughtful.

"You know, Riccardo's always been too smooth, too perfect. In business school, he was the guy who never seemed to sweat, never seemed to struggle." He paused, swirling his whiskey. "But lately, he's been different. More on edge. I've heard rumours..."

"What kind of rumours?" Allegra asked.

"The kind you hear in certain circles. Private poker games, high-stakes betting, associations with people his father wouldn't approve of." Nikolai pulled out his phone. "I have contacts who move in those circles. People who owe me favours."

"You're talking about investigating Riccardo Rossini," Allegra said slowly. "That's dangerous if the wrong people discover what you're doing."

"So is letting him blackmail you into marriage," Mishka pointed out. "And if he's got secrets worth hiding, maybe we can turn his own game against him."

Nikolai was already scrolling through his contacts. "Give me forty-eight hours. If Riccardo's got skeletons in his closet, I'll find them."

Allegra looked between Mishka and her brother, seeing determination in both their faces. For the first time since Riccardo's threats, she felt a flicker of hope. She hadn't had much to do with Nikolai before this, but already she was beginning to like him. Brother and sister had admirable qualities.

"All right," she said quietly. "Let's see what Riccardo Rossini is really hiding."

***

The meetings for *Harbour Light* had become both a blessing and a torment. What had initially been something Allegra wanted to avoid—working closely with her father—had transformed into her lifeline, the only legitimate reason she could continue seeing Mishka without raising suspicions. But the strain of pretending they were merely business associates was becoming unbearable.

Allegra sat at the polished conference table, forcing herself to focus on the architectural plans spread before them while hyperaware of Mishka's presence three seats away. Every gesture, every professional comment, every carefully neutral glance felt like a performance. The weight of their secret pressed down on her chest, making it difficult to breathe.

"The spa facilities need to be completely reimagined," Mishka was saying, her voice crisp and professional. "Current luxury standards demand much more than what we're seeing in these preliminary designs."

Riccardo leaned back in his chair, that insufferable smirk playing at the corners of his mouth. "I'm sure the ladies will have plenty of opinions about that," he said, his tone just patronizing enough to make Allegra's jaw clench. "After all, women know what women want, don't they?"

He caught Allegra's eye across the table, and she saw the calculation there. He thought he had her exactly where he wanted her—trapped in this charade, with no way out. His confidence was maddening, the way he sat there so smugly, as if their eventual engagement was a foregone conclusion.

Allegra forced a polite smile. "I'm sure we'll all contribute valuable perspectives to the project."

From the corner of her eye, she noticed Nikolai watching them with that sharp, analytical gaze of his. Had he picked up on the undercurrents in the room? The way she and Mishka seemed to gravitate toward each other, the careful way they avoided prolonged eye contact, the tension that had nothing to do with business disagreements?

Dangerous Liaisons

The meeting dragged on, each minute feeling like an hour. When they finally broke for lunch, Allegra lingered, pretending to review the contracts while her father and Franco discussed steel and concrete supplies. Riccardo excused himself to make phone calls, leaving just enough space for her to breathe.

***

Later that evening, in the quiet of her father's study, Gianni Castelli poured himself a scotch and settled into his leather chair. The amber liquid caught the lamplight as he studied his daughter over the rim of his glass.

"What do you think of Riccardo?" he asked without preamble.

Allegra had been expecting this conversation, but her stomach still knotted. "He's... competent. Knows the business."

"That's not what I meant, and you know it." Her father's voice was gentle but firm. "Franco's been a good friend for years, Allegra. Our businesses are closely intertwined. It makes sense that our relationship should be confirmed in more personal ways."

She kept her expression carefully neutral. "I see."

"He's a good-looking man. Intelligent. Comes from good stock." Gianni swirled his scotch thoughtfully. "A relationship with him wouldn't be a hardship. And after all, there are no other men in your life."

No, and there won't be. There's a beautiful, sexy woman, and with her by my side, I'll never want anything else.

But she couldn't say that. The words burned in her throat, but she swallowed them down. Her father and the family would never accept that she loved a woman. Franco would be focused on the grandsons he hoped she would bear, the continuation of bloodlines and business empires.

"I'm not opposed to the idea," she lied smoothly. "I just think we should take things slowly. Make sure we're compatible."

Gianni nodded approvingly. "Wise. Though don't take too long, cara mia. Opportunity doesn't wait forever."

***

The next consortium meeting was scheduled at the Empire flagship hotel. Allegra's pulse quickened when Mishka suggested she give her a tour of their existing facilities, to better understand their design philosophy.

"That's an excellent idea," Riccardo interjected before Allegra could respond. "I might come along. Get a sense of your operational standards."

Mishka's smile was perfectly professional. "Of course, though I should warn you, we'll be discussing fabrics and colour schemes, interior design elements. Very detailed decorating decisions."

Riccardo's expression shifted to one of mild disdain. "Women's stuff," he said with a dismissive wave. "Count me out. I'll review the financial projections instead."

The moment they were out of earshot, both women broke into barely suppressed laughter.

Dangerous Liaisons

"Women's stuff?" Mishka whispered, her eyes dancing with mischief.

"His loss," Allegra murmured, allowing herself to really look at Mishka for the first time all day. The careful professional mask slipped, revealing the warmth and desire underneath.

Mishka led her through the opulent lobby, past the main elevators to a private lift that required a key card. "Presidential Suite," she explained quietly. "Complete privacy. Spa facilities, small infinity pool, fully stocked bar."

The elevator doors whispered open, revealing a suite that shimmered with restrained opulence—sleek marble floors, velvet furnishings, a view of the city like a glittering promise. But Allegra barely noticed. Her attention was fixed on Mishka, whose eyes had shifted from businesslike calm to something hungry, intent.

Allegra stepped inside. The doors slid shut behind them.

Then Mishka was on her.

"I've been thinking about binging you here since the moment you walked into that first meeting," she whispered, backing Allegra toward the floor-to-ceiling window, her lips grazing Allegra's ear. "All those tailored dresses. The way you tilt your head when you're listening. You don't even realize what you do to me."

Their mouths collided, lips parting, tongues sliding together in a kiss that felt more like possession than invitation. Allegra moaned softly, clutching Mishka's waist, pulling her closer. Mishka's thigh slipped between hers and pressed—just enough to make Allegra shudder.

"God, yes," Allegra whispered, her breath hitching. "I've been thinking about you all through that meeting."

"Then let me give you what you want," Mishka breathed, hands already working the buttons of Allegra's blouse with single-minded urgency. "Let me *ruin* you for anyone else."

The blouse fell away. Mishka's mouth was on her throat, then lower, tongue tracing the line between silk and skin. She pulled the lace cup of Allegra's bra down with her teeth, then circled a nipple with her tongue until it peaked. She sucked gently, then harder, until Allegra gasped and clutched at her hair.

They stumbled to the sofa, peeling away layers, kisses deepening, bodies pressing closer. Mishka's hands roamed freely now—firm and confident—sliding along Allegra's hips, her thighs, stroking the skin above her stockings like a painter reverent with brushstrokes.

"Does Riccardo even know how to touch you?" Mishka asked, voice low, dark. "Will he ever know how to make you beg?"

"No," Allegra moaned, arching as Mishka's fingers slid beneath her panties. "Only you. Only you can make me feel like this."

Mishka kissed her again, deeper, then whispered against her lips, "Then let me hear you."

She slid two fingers inside, curling just right, her thumb brushing the aching spot that made Allegra cry out, head falling back, thighs trembling. Mishka moved slowly at first, watching her unravel, then faster, stroking deeper, relentless and tender all at once.

Dangerous Liaisons

Allegra's body bucked beneath her, hands scrambling for something to hold on to—her wrist, her waist, anything. Her climax built like fire in her belly, spreading outward, coiling tighter.

"Look at me," Mishka said, and when Allegra's eyes fluttered open, Mishka kissed her hard—just as Allegra shattered in her hand with a cry that echoed off the glass.

She collapsed into Mishka's arms, breath ragged, skin damp, heart pounding. But Mishka wasn't done. She guided Allegra gently onto her back, trailing kisses down her belly, pausing just above the ache between her thighs. Allegra tensed, then moaned as Mishka's tongue replaced her fingers, slow and deliberate, her hands gripping Allegra's hips as if anchoring her to this moment.

Every stroke, every flick, every suck pulled Allegra higher again. The view outside blurred to nothing. The only thing real was the woman between her legs, the sounds she coaxed from her, the molten pressure building again, impossibly.

"I want you in my bed every night," Mishka said between kisses. "Your body, your voice, your soul."

Allegra came again, harder this time—crying out Mishka's name, her legs shaking, hands tangled in Mishka's hair. When it passed, she pulled Mishka up and kissed her, tasting herself on her lover's lips.

And then it was Allegra's turn.

She pushed Mishka back against the cushions, straddling her thighs, eyes blazing. "You think I'm the one who forgets who I am," she said, voice husky. "But you? You need to know what it's like to be wanted. *Worshipped.*"

She kissed her way down Mishka's body, taking her time. Biting gently at her breasts, dragging her tongue across Mishka's stomach until the woman beneath her trembled, one hand over her eyes, the other fisting the cushion.

Allegra slipped a hand between Mishka's legs, finding her soaked and ready, then replaced fingers with mouth, tongue pressing deep, flicking hard, then slow, learning the shape of her pleasure. Mishka came with a sharp gasp, then again, legs locked around Allegra's shoulders, riding wave after wave until she collapsed, boneless and breathless.

They lay tangled together, limbs entwined, sweat cooling on skin that still tingled from too much pleasure.

And still, Allegra couldn't stop touching her. Stroking her spine. Pressing soft kisses to her shoulder.

"Promise me this won't just be a stolen moment," she whispered.

Mishka opened her eyes, raw and honest. "No. This is real. You and me. Whatever it takes… I want all of it. It's not just the sex. I want you to understand that. I want you by m side, Alegra Castelli… always."

Outside, the city moved on. But in this private world they'd created, nothing else existed but desire, devotion, and a love too powerful to keep pretending.

Chapter 9

THREE DAYS LATER, they met in Nikolai's apartment—a penthouse that spoke of new money trying very hard to look old. Mishka had chosen it because it was clean, meaning no bugs, no surveillance, no family obligations listening in.

"Tell me you found something," Allegra said without preamble. She looked tired, older somehow, as if Riccardo's threats had aged her overnight.

Mishka spread a manila folder across the coffee table like she was dealing cards. "Oh, we found something all right. Several somethings."

Nikolai cracked his knuckles, settling back into the leather couch. "Turns out pretty boy Riccardo isn't as clean as he pretends to be. My contacts in the financial district were very chatty once I greased a few palms."

"Start with the gambling," Mishka prompted.

"Right. So, Riccardo has a serious problem with poker. Not the friendly Friday night kind—the kind where you lose six figures in a single evening and keep coming back for more." Nikolai pulled out a series of photographs showing

Riccardo at various underground games. "These are from the past three months alone."

Allegra studied the images. In each one, Riccardo looked increasingly desperate, his usually perfect composure cracking around the edges.

"How much?" she asked.

"Conservative estimate? He's down about two million. And that's just what my guy could track. Could be more."

Mishka nodded grimly. "Which explains why he's so desperate to marry into money. Your dowry would cover his debts and then some."

"But that's not the best part," Nikolai continued, clearly enjoying himself. "The best part is who he owes money to."

He pulled out another photograph, this one showing Riccardo in heated conversation with a man Allegra didn't recognize—thin, sharp-featured, with the kind of pale eyes that suggested violence was never far from the surface.

"Viktor Antonov," Nikolai said. "Russian mob. Not the kind of people you want to owe money to, and definitely not the kind of people Riccardo's father would approve of him doing business with."

"The Rossinis have always prided themselves on keeping their operations purely Italian," Mishka added. "Old school traditions, family honour, all that. If Frank Rossini found out his heir was in bed with the Russians..."

"He'd be furious," Allegra finished, understanding dawning on her face. "But this is all circumstantial. Photos of him at poker games, meeting with questionable people. It's not enough to—"

"Which is why we also have this." Mishka produced a small digital recorder. "Courtesy of Nikolai's contact at the Antonov organization."

"You recorded him?" Allegra's eyes widened.

"Viktor likes to keep records of his business dealings," Nikolai explained. "Insurance, you might say. He was happy to share a copy in exchange for some information about Castelli shipping routes."

Mishka pressed play. Riccardo's voice filled the room, slightly distorted but unmistakably him:

"I need more time. I'll be able to set a wedding date soon, and once that's done—"

"Next month is too long," came Viktor's accented reply. *"My patience grows thin, Riccardo Rossini. Two million dollars is not pocket change, even for families like yours."*

"You'll get your money. I just need Allegra's cooperation. Once we're married, I'll take control of her trust fund. It's a guaranteed return on your investment."

"And if she refuses?"

"She won't refuse. I'll make sure of that."

The recording continued for several more minutes, Riccardo's voice growing more desperate, more specific about his plans to manipulate Allegra into marriage. By the end, there was no doubt about his motivations or his methods.

"Jesus," Allegra breathed. "He really sees me as nothing more than a financial transaction."

"Now you have leverage," Mishka said, ejecting the recording device. "Riccardo threatens your family, you threaten to expose his gambling debts and Russian connections to his father. Mutually assured destruction."

"But will it be enough?" Allegra asked. "Riccardo's desperate. Desperate people do unpredictable things."

"There's some more information you can leverage," Nikolai said, not bothering to hide his gleeful grin. "What will his father say about his son dipping his wick where it doesn't belong?"

"What do you mean?"

Nikolai slid another photo across the table. It showed Riccardo standing at the front of an apartment. A young woman stood in the doorway, with a young child on her hip. In the next photo, he leaned forward to kiss her.

"This is Elena, his mistress and their son. Riccardo has been a very deceitful boy. What will papa think about that?"

***

The morning sun cast long shadows across the marble steps of the Belmont Hotel as Allegra approached the entrance. She had chosen this neutral ground carefully—public enough to ensure safety, private enough for the conversation that needed to happen. Her heart hammered against her ribs, but her expression remained composed. This was a chess game, and she intended to win.

As she walked through the lobby, she caught sight of Tony pretending to read a newspaper near the concierge desk. His surveillance had become almost comically obvious over the past week. She paused beside his chair, offering a sardonic smile.

"Want me to tell you where I'm going today, Tony? Saves you the bother of having to follow me."

Tony's newspaper crinkled as his grip tightened, but he didn't look up. "Don't know what you're talking about, Miss Allegra."

"Of course you don't." She patted his shoulder with mock affection. "Third floor, private dining room. In case you need to update your reports."

Riccardo was already seated when she arrived, his usual swagger subdued but his jaw set in that familiar stubborn line. He'd chosen a seat facing the door—always the strategist, always looking for an exit. The private dining room felt smaller with his presence filling it, tension crackling between them like electricity before a storm.

"This is unexpected," he said, not bothering to stand. "Though I have to say, the mysterious invitation was intriguing."

Allegra took the seat across from him, maintaining eye contact. "We need to talk, Riccardo. About your extracurricular activities."

His laugh was sharp, cutting. "If this is about wedding planning, I think you're jumping the gun. We haven't even—"

"Viktor Antonov."

The name dropped between them like a stone into still water. Riccardo's face went very still, the practiced charm falling away to reveal something harder, more dangerous underneath.

"I don't know what you think you know—"

"I know about the gambling debts. The Russian connections. The money you owe to people who don't accept late payments." Allegra kept her voice steady, professional. "I also know about the woman. And the child."

Riccardo's knuckles went white as he gripped the edge of the table. "You've been busy."

"Someone had to be. You're stirring up trouble that goes far beyond your own life, Riccardo. Our families are connected whether we like it or not. Your mess becomes everyone's mess."

"And what exactly do you think you can do about it?" His voice dropped to a whisper, but there was venom in it. "Threaten me? Blackmail me?"

"I'm offering you a deal." Allegra leaned forward slightly. "You publicly declare you're not interested in pursuing this marriage arrangement. Make it clear to both our families that you don't want to move forward. In exchange, I keep your secrets."

"My secrets?" Riccardo's laugh was bitter. "You mean the gambling? The fact that I've been haemorrhaging money at the Volkov family's casino? Or are you talking about Elena and Milly?"

The names hung in the air. His mistress and daughter, Allegra realized. Not just abstract concepts anymore, but real people whose lives would be destroyed if his father learned the truth.

"All of it," she said quietly. "But this doesn't solve your fundamental problem, Riccardo. You still owe money to dangerous people. You still have responsibilities you're hiding from."

He sat up straighter, eyes flashing his barely suppressed anger. "That's my problem to solve."

"See that you do. It becomes my family's problem when those dangerous people start looking for leverage. When they decide your father's business connections might be useful. When they realize the Rossinis have ties that could be exploited."

Riccardo was quiet for a long moment, staring out the window at the city below. When he finally spoke, his voice was different—tired, almost defeated.

"You think you're so smart, don't you? Coming in here with your research and your ultimatums."

"I think I'm practical. And I think you're in over your head."

"Fine." The word came out like a curse. "I'll call off the engagement talks. Tell my father I've reconsidered, that I don't think we're compatible." His eyes met hers, and there was nothing but cold fury there. "But don't think this ends here, Allegra. Don't think you can manipulate me and walk away clean."

The threat was clear, hanging between them like a blade. Allegra felt a chill run down her spine, but she kept her expression neutral.

"I'm not trying to manipulate you, Riccardo. I'm trying to give us both a way out of an impossible situation."

"Is that what you call it?" He stood abruptly, the chair scraping against the floor. "You've just made an enemy, Allegra. I hope you're prepared for the consequences."

He left without another word, the door closing behind him with a soft click that somehow sounded more ominous than if he'd slammed it.

Allegra sat alone in the dining room for several minutes with her hands folded carefully in her lap. She'd gotten what she wanted—Riccardo would end the engagement talks, freeing her from a marriage of convenience she never wanted. But his parting words echoed in her mind.

She had made an enemy today. A desperate, dangerous enemy with connections to the Russian mafia and nothing left to lose. Riccardo wouldn't disappear quietly into the night. He'd find ways to cause trouble, to seek his revenge.

As she finally stood to leave, Allegra made a mental note to speak with Nikolai about increasing security measures. The game was far from over, and Riccardo had just shown her exactly how ruthless he could be when cornered.

The real battle was just beginning.

Chapter 10

MISHKA'S APARTMENT HAD become their sanctuary. Where Allegra's family home simmered with watchful eyes, polite silences, and the heavy air of unspoken expectations, this place offered them space to simply *be*. In the penthouse high above the harbour, they could breathe freely—no questions, no obligations, no pretending.

The apartment itself, a lavish twenty-first birthday gift from Mikhail Antonov to his only daughter, reflected Mishka's refinement and her father's indulgence. He'd always admired her sharp intellect, even if he didn't always understand her choices. He believed in her brilliance, and this space—sleek, modern, and perfectly private—was proof.

Good Italian girls lived with their families until marriage. That tradition, once sacred to Allegra's mother, felt to Allegra like a polished cage. Every deviation from that path—her ambition, her love for Mishka—was another crack in the mask she wore for her family. In Mishka's world, the cage didn't exist. Here, they were equals, co-conspirators, lovers. Free.

It was because of this she plucked up the courage to look for a rental apartment. It had to be close to the city, her father's office, and of course, to Mishka. She found one with harbour views, and a fabulous wrap-around balcony. Only when the lease was signed did she tell Gianni she was moving.

"You have a home here with everything you need. It's also fully secure. A daughter's place is at home with her family. This is where you need to live, with me. Who will look after you in some strange place?"

"Papa, I managed perfectly well in London, and that was on the other side of the world. This is the twenty-first century. Women live in their own apartments now."

They still argued about it, but in the end, Gianni agreed, but only after he had sent his security specialist around to check out the property, and to add cameras, lights, and monitoring devices. On the one hand, Allegra thought it was over the top, but on the other, remembering Riccardo's fury with her, it was reassuring.

Spending time in Mishka's apartment, removed from her father's monitoring, still remained her preference. After unpacking and settling into her new apartment, she drove over to spend the evening with Mishka, complete with a spare key for her new sanctuary.

They dined first at the restaurant on the ground floor—La Piazetta, all dim lighting and impeccable service. They sat at a corner booth, sharing wood-fired pizza with smoked scamorza and rocket, plates of marinated artichokes, and a bottle of Montepulciano. They laughed over small things—blunders from Allegra's morning meeting, Mishka's dry commentary on her father's latest investment—yet their feet remained pressed together under the table, a quiet affirmation of everything unspoken.

By the time they returned to the apartment, the city had begun its slow descent into night. They tossed off heels and slipped into soft knits, clearing the dining table to spread out architectural sketches, printouts, and business notes. Between sips of wine and the scratching of pens, they crafted the bones of the business concept they had previously discussed: *The Matilda*—a women-only luxury hotel that balanced security, comfort, and quiet strength.

"The first floor can be dedicated to a business suite," Mishka said, her finger gliding across the floorplan. "Private boardrooms, maybe co-working lounges. And the rooftop…" Her lips curved as she looked up. "Skydeck massage lounges. City views. Glass of champers in hand. Sun setting behind the skyline."

Allegra smiled, tapping her teeth with the end of her pen. "Sounds like my ideal. But we need discrete security. Women travelling alone should feel… cocooned. Safe without being watched."

Mishka nodded. "Private keycard lifts, monitored entries, concierge-level background checks. No male staff above the first floor."

Their fingers brushed as they reached for the same page of costings, and the contact sent a spark through Allegra's chest. They lingered just a moment too long, eyes locking.

"The business plan's solid," Mishka murmured, voice low, eyes darker now. "But you're the real reason I love working on it."

"Same," Allegra whispered, setting her pen down slowly. "Though if we keep getting distracted, we'll never launch the thing."

Mishka grinned and leaned forward, brushing her lips over Allegra's knuckles. "Let it take time. We've waited this long."

Later, they moved to the balcony, wine glasses in hand, the harbour spread out beneath them like a velvet painting. The salty wind tangled Allegra's hair as she leaned into Mishka's warmth. Their hips touched, and the city sparkled in silent witness.

"Sometimes," Allegra said quietly, "I imagine what it would feel like to just… exist. Not hide. To hold your hand in the middle of the day and not care who sees."

Mishka reached for her hand, weaving their fingers together. "We'll find a way. Maybe not today. Maybe not tomorrow. But eventually."

Their kiss was soft and certain, born of trust and longing—until something in the distance caught Allegra's eye. A pinpoint reflection. Glass on glass. Too deliberate to ignore.

Her breath caught. "Don't react," she whispered against Mishka's lips. "We're being watched."

Mishka stilled, only her eyes moving. "Where?"

"Across the street. Rooftop level. Camera lens. Tony's watching us."

The name landed like a dropped stone.

Mishka's voice was barely audible. "Riccardo's getting nervous."

Dangerous Liaisons

"Desperate," Allegra corrected, her mind already racing. "He wants proof. Leverage. This stops tonight."

They didn't move suddenly—just leaned back with practiced ease, sipping their wine as if nothing had changed. A moment later, they slipped inside through the sliding glass doors, eyes no longer on each other, but on escape.

Inside, Mishka set down her glass. "There's a boat," she said quietly. "Family cruiser. Moored at the private jetty. It's clean. No tracking. If we can get Tony there…"

"Away from the cameras. From witnesses." Allegra's voice was steady, her body electric with adrenaline. "You go. Get the engine running. I'll bring him."

Mishka grabbed Allegra's arm, her grip fierce. "Are you sure?"

"I don't want to be." She looked into Mishka's eyes. "But if we let him keep watching, he'll destroy everything."

There was a beat of silence between them—filled with fear, resolve, and something deeper: *the knowledge that once they crossed this line, there was no going back.*

Mishka's jaw set. "I'll wait for your signal."

Allegra nodded, eyes already flicking toward her bag and the burner phone she carried when staying at Mishka's apartment tucked inside. Her voice, when she spoke again, was low and final.

"Tonight, we end it."

***

Allegra crossed the street with measured steps, heart hammering in her chest. Her hands were steady, but only because she had made them so. She spotted the familiar grey sedan parked in the shadows, the lens of the telephoto camera still aimed up at Mishka's balcony like a silent weapon.

She knocked once, sharply, on the passenger window.

Tony jolted, nearly dropping the camera. His wide eyes met hers through the glass—recognition, then panic. He scrambled to roll the window down.

"Hello, Tony," Allegra said smoothly, her voice sugar-laced steel. "Long time no see."

"Miss Allegra, I don't know what you think you're—"

"Cut the act." She opened the door and slid into the passenger seat uninvited, the scent of stale coffee and sweat thick in the car. "Show me what you've got."

Tony hesitated, clutching the camera protectively to his chest. But he saw the cool determination in her eyes—something final—and slowly, reluctantly, turned the screen toward her. He scrolled through the images, each one a silent betrayal: her and Mishka on the balcony, their hands brushing, bodies leaning together, a kiss that had felt safe in the moment but now made her stomach twist.

It wasn't just surveillance. It was violation.

"I got audio too," Tony said, finding his swagger again as he saw her face tighten. "Laser mic. Picked up some very interesting stuff. About your *relationship*, sure, but also your little hotel idea. The Matilda, right? Feminist paradise. Bet the papers would love that. So would your family."

Her voice was ice. "What do you want?"

Dangerous Liaisons

"Riccardo's paying me well," Tony said, smug now. "But you? Maybe you'd like to make a better offer. Say, fifty thousand, and I delete the lot. Walk away."

She forced herself to nod slowly, as if considering. "That's a lot of money to carry around."

"I can be patient," he said. "But not too patient. Let's not pretend Riccardo isn't watching you like a hawk."

Allegra darted her eyes nervously to the street, playing her part. "Fine. I'll have to do a bank transfer. Meet me at the private jetty behind the building. No cameras there. No one listening in."

Tony smirked. "Ten minutes."

***

The private marina was cloaked in shadow, the only illumination the occasional sweep of light from the harbour patrol in the distance. The water lapped quietly at the pylons, masking the low hum of the cruiser's engine.

Mishka stood at the helm, dark hair tied back, her features unreadable. The boat was sleek, expensive, and ready.

When Tony emerged from the shadows, his camera bag slung over one shoulder, his pace slowed.

"What about the money?" he demanded, voice sharper now, eyes scanning the water.

"On the boat," Allegra replied with a calm she didn't feel. "We can talk privately."

He hesitated. Then stepped aboard. Allegra released the breath she'd been holding.

The engine deepened in tone as Mishka eased them away from the dock. The city lights faded behind them, swallowed by the inky black of the harbour. Allegra stood beside Tony on the rear deck, watching him out of the corner of her eye. He was getting twitchy.

"This is far enough," Tony said after a few minutes, shifting on his feet. "Let's just get this over with."

Mishka didn't respond. The boat kept moving.

Tony turned sharply. "Hey—I said *this is far enough!*"

Allegra stepped between him and the wheelhouse. "No, Tony. It's not."

He froze. "What the hell is this?"

"Insurance," she said. "We're far enough from shore that no one's listening. No one's watching. You know that my father has eyes and ears everywhere. Now we can be honest."

He snorted, but there was a flicker of fear in his eyes. "You think you're scaring me? You don't have the stomach for this."

"Don't I?" Her voice was soft. "You've been stalking me. Spying on us. Recording conversations you had no right to hear. You were going to blackmail us—for money or worse."

Tony's smirk faltered. "Riccardo already has copies. You touch me, and you'll regret it."

"No, he doesn't," Mishka said from the helm, her voice razor-sharp. "If he did, he would've acted by now."

"Besides," Allegra added, stepping closer, "you're a liar, Tony. You always have been. We know you've been playing both sides. Hoping to sell to whoever offered more."

His bluff crumbled. He lunged toward the radio controls near the wheelhouse—pure instinct, a last-ditch play.

"Stop him!" Allegra shouted.

The boat rocked violently as Mishka cut the engine. Tony stumbled, grabbed the railing, then pivoted toward the controls again. Allegra tackled him. They crashed against the deck, a flailing tangle of limbs. He swung at her—wild, desperate. She ducked, elbowed him hard in the ribs. Mishka was there in a second, grabbing his arm, wrenching the camera bag off his shoulder.

He shoved her away and lunged for the rail. For a split second, Allegra thought he might jump, might swim for it.

But the boat listed with a swell and Tony lost his footing. His hand missed the rail. He tumbled into the water with a splash that echoed across the harbour.

"Tony!" Allegra yelled, moving to the edge. But there was no answer. No head breaking the surface. No sound but the steady slap of the waves against the hull.

The camera bag followed seconds later—slipped from Mishka's hands, or maybe tossed. It hit the water with a soft splash and sank.

They waited.

Still, nothing.

Allegra's hands were shaking. Mishka said nothing, only restarted the engine and turned the boat toward shore.

***

The journey back was silent except for the motor's low hum and the distant, indifferent sounds of the sleeping city. Allegra leaned against the rail, wind in her hair, her heart thudding with too many emotions to name.

They docked without speaking. Mishka tied off the mooring rope, her hands steady as if she hadn't just witnessed a man vanish into the dark.

"There's no going back from this," she said at last, her voice low.

"No," Allegra agreed. "There isn't."

They walked back toward the building, side by side. At the entrance, their hands brushed. Mishka didn't pull away.

In the elevator, they stood in silence. Allegra caught her reflection in the polished steel doors. Her face looked the same—eyes calm, mouth set—but she knew what she was now. What they were.

She turned her hand over, finding Mishka's fingers, curling them into hers.

There would be fallout. Consequences. A future altered by one irreversible night.

But for now, there was this: the woman she loved beside her, the secret between them buried in dark water, and the whisper of relief that she had finally stopped running.

Chapter 11

THE WEIGHT OF expectation sat on Allegra's shoulders as she walked through the marble corridors of Castelli Enterprises toward her office. Every step echoed her father's dreams for her, dreams that felt more like chains with each passing day. Her MBA had been meant to prepare her for this moment—taking her place as heir to the family empire—but all it had done was show her how many other paths existed beyond these walls.

She paused outside her father's office, watching through the glass as Gianni pored over shipping manifests with the same intense focus he'd brought to everything since she was a child. He'd built this company from nothing, using street smarts and sheer determination to compensate for the formal education he'd never received. Now he was counting on her sophisticated business training to take them to the next level.

The irony wasn't lost on her. He needed her expertise to legitimize operations that had always straddled the line between legal and illegal. The tobacco and alcohol imports that had funded her privileged upbringing, her education, her opportunities—she knew better than to ask too many questions about the details. But she also knew she didn't want to be the one to carry that legacy forward.

The knock was soft, but insistent. "Come in," Allegra called, her voice flat with the weight of everything she hadn't said to her father.

The door opened just wide enough for Enrico to slip inside. Always neat, always measured, he moved like a man who knew exactly how much space he was entitled to occupy—and never an inch more. He closed the door quietly behind him, his movements calm, deliberate.

"Rico," she said, raising an eyebrow. "Shouldn't you be off charming suppliers or shaking down customs officers?"

"Funny." He gave a faint smile, the kind that never quite reached his eyes. "I figured you might be in the mood for honesty today."

He crossed to the chair opposite her desk and settled in with the grace of someone used to waiting, watching. She saw the family resemblance more sharply in moments like this: the sharp jawline, the eyes that missed nothing, the stillness that could turn predatory without warning.

"You look like you're attending your own funeral every time you walk in here," he said, cutting straight to the point.

She leaned back, folding her arms. "You came in here to offer fashion advice?"

"No," he said coolly. "I came in here to talk about the fact that Uncle Gianni is planning to announce your promotion next month."

Allegra froze. "He's what?"

Dangerous Liaisons

"Second in Command. Full partnership track. Your own division, starting with the South American logistics—he thinks it's a proving ground. I hear he's already speaking to his lawyer about revising the trust structure."

Her stomach twisted. South America. That wasn't just logistics—it was code for the greyer parts of the operation, the ones that had made Castelli Enterprises rich, and untouchable. She felt the floor tilt under her.

"Of course he is," she murmured bitterly. "Nothing says 'I love you, daughter' like throwing you into the deep end of an international smuggling operation."

Enrico gave a low chuckle, the sound dry as dust. "You always did have a gift for phrasing."

She studied him, noticing the ease with which he delivered the news—like someone who'd had time to process it, maybe even plan around it. And that's when she saw it: the gleam behind his steady gaze. Hunger. A lifetime of second place curdling into something sharper.

"You want it," she said.

"I always have," he replied, unblinking.

"And yet he picked me."

Enrico shrugged, though the movement was tight around his shoulders. "You have the pedigree. The right degrees, the right polish. You don't just speak the language of money—you speak the dialect of legitimacy. That matters now."

"And what—you think I should just hand it over to you?"

"I think," he said, his voice quiet and measured, "that you should walk away if it's killing you. And I think I should be standing close enough to catch what you drop."

She stood abruptly and walked to the window. Far below, the city glittered with wealth and opportunity, each light a reminder of what had been built on risk, on blurred lines and blood ties.

"My father will never forgive me," she said.

"He'll be furious," Enrico agreed, standing as well. "But he won't stay furious forever. Especially if the family's still in good hands."

She turned to face him. "And you'd be the good hands?"

"I'm not you," he said with a shrug. "But I know this business. I've been loyal. I've done the jobs no one else wanted, with no spotlight. I've earned it, Allegra."

She hesitated, the years pressing in—birthday parties where Enrico watched her unwrap gifts his father could never afford for him, family dinners where she was praised while he was tolerated, always the understudy. Always patient.

"I'm not saying yes," she said finally. "But I'm listening."

"That's all I need—for now." He buttoned his jacket, his expression smoothing into something close to gratitude. "Just don't wait too long. Once the announcement is made, it'll be hard for either of us to steer the ship another way."

As he reached for the door, she stopped him. "Rico."

He paused, hand on the knob.

"If you're playing me—if this is some long game—"

"It's not," he said, turning his head. "But if you don't want the crown, cousin, don't be surprised if someone else wears it better. I think you should do what makes you happy. And I think I should have the chance to prove myself." His eyes met hers steadily. "We can help each other, Allegra."

Dangerous Liaisons

The office fell silent except for the distant hum of traffic far below. Allegra's mind raced through possibilities, complications, the delicate family dynamics that would need to be navigated.

"He'll be devastated," she said finally.

"He'll be angry. But he'll get over it if there's a suitable alternative." Enrico stood, straightening his tie. "Think about it. But don't think too long. Once he makes that announcement, backing out becomes much more complicated."

And with that, he slipped out, leaving her alone with the city lights and the sound of her father's empire ticking toward a decision she no longer wanted to make.

***

Three days later, Allegra arranged to meet Enrico at a small café in Neutral Bay, far from the family's usual haunts. She'd spent the intervening time wrestling with guilt, relief, and the terrifying prospect of disappointing the man who'd sacrificed everything for her future.

But she'd also spent time with Mishka, talking through options and possibilities, feeling her resolve strengthen with each conversation about their shared dreams for the hotel business.

"I want out," she said without preamble as Enrico joined her at a corner table. "But I need your help to make it happen without destroying my relationship with papa."

Enrico's smile was genuinely warm. "What do you need?"

"Time. A transition period where you can prove yourself indispensable. And eventually, his blessing for both of us to follow our own paths."

"Sounds reasonable. What's your timeline?"

"Six months. Maybe less if you can convince him that the company needs someone who's fully committed." She paused, studying his face. "You are fully committed, aren't you, Rico? Because if you're planning to use this as a stepping stone to something else—"

"This is what I want, Allegra. This company, this life. It's all I've ever wanted."

Something in his tone made her believe him. "Good. Because there's something else."

She'd debated whether to have this conversation, but if she was going to trust Enrico with her future, he needed to understand the stakes.

"There's someone I'd like you to meet. Someone who's... important to me. Her name is Mishka."

Enrico's eyebrows rose slightly, but he remained silent, letting her continue.

"She's brilliant. Extensive hospitality experience. We're working on some business ventures together."

"Just business?" The question was casual, but Allegra caught the knowing look in his eyes.

She met his gaze steadily. "That's all you need to know right now."

The silence stretched between them, filled with unspoken understanding. Enrico's expression cycled through calculation, surprise, and finally, something that looked like opportunity.

Dangerous Liaisons

"I see," he said carefully. "And Uncle Gianni?"

"Doesn't know. Can't know. Not yet." Allegra's voice was firm. "If you want my support for a larger role in the company, this stays between us. Completely confidential."

"He'll want grandsons eventually," Enrico said quietly.

"That's a bridge I'll cross when I come to it." She leaned forward slightly. "Do we have an understanding, Rico?"

Enrico nodded slowly. "You know, this might actually work in our favour."

"How do you figure?"

"He'll need someone to carry on the family traditions. Someone who can give him the grandsons he's dreaming of. Someone who can be the son he always wanted." Enrico's smile was calculating now. "Someone like me."

Allegra felt a chill of unease. "Rico, I'm not abandoning the family. I still have my shares, my voting rights. I'll still be involved in major decisions."

Enrico nodded slowly, understanding the terms of their arrangement. "Of course. And I'll need your support when your father considers expanding my role." He reached across the table to squeeze her hand. "We're family, Allegra. We look out for each other. Your secret is safe with me. And you'll have my vote of confidence when the time comes."

"Good." She extended her hand across the table. "Then we have a deal."

But as they shook hands to seal their agreement, Allegra couldn't shake the feeling that she was setting something in motion that she might not be able to control. Enrico's ambition was a powerful force, and she was about to give it free rein.

The question was whether she'd be able to trust him with her father's legacy—and her own secrets.

As they parted ways outside the café, Enrico turned back to her with a thoughtful expression. "When do I get to meet this Mishka?"

"Soon," Allegra said carefully. "But discretely. And Rico?" She paused, her voice taking on a warning tone. "If this gets back to papa before I'm ready..."

"It won't." His expression was serious now. "I understand what's at stake. For both of us."

She watched him walk away, hoping she could trust those words. Because she was about to put her future—and her heart—in the hands of someone whose loyalty she could only hope to count on.

***

The following week, Allegra stood outside Mishka's harborside apartment building, her arms folded tightly across her chest as she waited for the door to open. The air was crisp, and so was her anxiety. The conversation with Enrico had gone as well as she could have hoped—but the undercurrent of ambition in his tone still echoed in her mind. She needed him, yes, but she also needed to know where the fault lines were before they cracked beneath her.

The door swung open and she entered the foyer, making her way to the elevator. Mishka smiled, warm and welcoming, in that calming way she always had, as if nothing could touch her unless she allowed it.

Dangerous Liaisons

"You look like you've seen a ghost," Mishka said, ushering her inside.

"Close enough," Allegra muttered, dropping her coat onto a chair and accepting the glass of wine offered.

Mishka waited until they were both seated. "So? How did it go?"

"He agreed. More than agreed. He's... enthusiastic."

"That's good, right?"

Allegra hesitated. "It should be. But I'm not naïve. Enrico's waited his whole life to be seen. I just gave him the spotlight."

"And now you're wondering what he'll do once the lights are on."

"Exactly." She took a sip of the wine, then set it down untouched. "I told him about you."

Mishka blinked. "All of it?"

"Not the details. Just that we're working together. That you're important to me."

A slow smile spread across Mishka's lips, tinged with caution. "And he took it... how?"

"Like a man processing leverage." Allegra leaned forward, elbows on her knees. "He didn't say anything overt. But I know that look. He's thinking two steps ahead already. Probably three."

Mishka was quiet for a long moment. "Do you think he'll use it against you?"

"I don't know. That's what terrifies me. I've just handed him a knife and asked him to help me cut ties—I'm not entirely sure he won't slip it between my ribs instead."

"Then don't give him the chance." Mishka leaned in. "Control the narrative. Set the tone. Introduce him to me on your terms."

Allegra looked at her, grateful for her clarity. "He asked to meet you."

Mishka's brows lifted. "Really?"

"I told him soon. Carefully. Quietly."

"Then let's plan it. Neutral ground. Keep it professional. You won't regret trusting me, Allegra." Her tone softened. "We've already started something. We can build it. Our way."

Allegra nodded slowly, feeling the warmth of possibility—just enough to push back the chill of uncertainty.

***

Two days later, the meeting was arranged. A boutique hotel bar in Darlinghurst, upscale and quiet, perfect for discretion. Enrico arrived first, immaculately dressed, carrying a bottle of wine wrapped in gold ribbon—a peace offering, or a message, Allegra wasn't sure.

Mishka joined them shortly after, poised, confident, dressed in soft linen and quiet power. She greeted Enrico with a firm handshake and a calm smile, every inch the business partner.

They talked shop at first. Hospitality trends. Investment opportunities. Global branding.

Allegra observed closely, trying to read between the lines. Enrico was charming—too charming—and she could see how easily he adapted to Mishka's intelligence, even admired it. But there was something else. A flicker of interest. The way he

Dangerous Liaisons

held her gaze just a little too long. The way his questions about her background veered subtly toward the personal.

After Mishka excused herself to take a call, Enrico leaned in toward Allegra.

"She's impressive," he said quietly.

"She is."

"Beautiful, too."

Allegra didn't rise to the bait. "She's my partner. In business. Possibly more."

"Does she know what she's getting into?" he asked, with a faint smirk. "What it means to be close to a Castelli?"

Allegra turned her head, slowly, until their eyes met. "She knows everything she needs to."

Enrico studied her for a beat longer, then nodded. "Understood."

But Allegra knew that look too. She'd seen it in boardrooms and backroom deals. He was filing Mishka away, categorizing her. Threat or asset? Leverage or liability?

Later, as they said their goodbyes outside the hotel, Enrico pulled Allegra aside while Mishka waited at the curb for a car.

"She's smart," he said. "And sharp. But be careful, cugina."

"Of what?"

"Of anyone who could cost you everything—before you've even had a chance to build it."

Allegra met his eyes. "Thanks for the advice. But I'm more worried about the people I do trust."

He gave her a slow, deliberate nod. "Then I hope I stay on that list."

Rowena Wylde

As he walked away, Allegra stood in the fading light, heart beating faster than she liked to admit. Because trusting Enrico was starting to feel less like a strategic alliance—and more like a gamble. And the stakes were rising.

Chapter 12

THE AFTERNOON SUN filtered through the silk curtains of Sofia Antonov's private sitting room, casting delicate patterns across the antique Persian rug. At eighty-three, Sofia still commanded the space around her like an empress, her silver hair perfectly coiffed, her posture ramrod straight despite her age. She sat behind a mahogany desk that had once belonged to her late husband, reviewing documents with the same sharp focus that had helped her navigate decades of family politics.

Mishka paused in the doorway, as she always did, taking in the sight of the woman who had been her greatest influence and fiercest protector. The room smelled of jasmine tea and the faint trace of Sofia's signature perfume—a scent that instantly transported Mishka back to childhood afternoons spent listening to stories of the old country.

"Baba," she said warmly, crossing the room to kiss her grandmother's papery cheek.

"Mishka, moya dorogaya," Sofia replied, her voice carrying the slight accent that decades in Australia had never quite erased. She gestured to the chair across from her desk. "Sit, sit. You look well. The harbour air agrees with you."

"Thank you for seeing me on such short notice."

Sofia waved a dismissive hand, her rings catching the light. "You never need an appointment with me, child. Now, tell me about this consortium business. The reports I've been receiving are promising, but I prefer to hear details from someone I trust."

Mishka settled into the familiar rhythm of business discussion, outlining the progress on the new hotel development. "The architectural plans are nearly finalized," she said, pulling documents from her briefcase. "We've secured the harbor-front location, and the initial environmental assessments are complete."

"And the Castellis? How are you finding them to work with?"

"Professional. Hungry for success. Aggressive investors. They have much to learn about the hospitality market, but they are keen." Mishka kept her voice carefully neutral, but she felt her grandmother's sharp eyes studying her face.

"The daughter—Allegra, is it? She is developing a reputation in business circles. Studied in London for her MBA, I believe."

"She's... very capable. Her insights have been invaluable."

Sofia leaned back in her chair, steepling her fingers. "The timeline for construction?"

"Eighteen months from ground breaking to opening the first phase. We're looking at a spring 2027 launch if everything stays on schedule."

"Excellent. The market conditions should be favourable by then." Sofia paused, her gaze never leaving Mishka's face.

"The profit projections are conservative—we could see returns of twenty to thirty percent above your estimates if we manage the positioning correctly."

They continued discussing details for another twenty minutes—staffing requirements, marketing strategies, potential partnerships with international hotel chains. But throughout the conversation, Mishka felt her grandmother's attention focused on something beyond the business at hand.

Finally, Sofia set down her tea cup with a delicate clink and fixed Mishka with that penetrating stare that had always seen straight through to the truth.

"That is all good news," she said, her voice taking on a knowing tone. "But I have read the reports your brother sends me. I think, perhaps, there is some other reason for you visiting today." She smiled, the expression both warm and calculating. "Your visits are always most welcome, of course, but now I sense there is an ulterior motive."

Mishka felt heat rise in her cheeks. Even at twenty-eight, she still felt like a child under her grandmother's scrutiny. "I... there is something else."

"Ah." Sofia's smile widened. "I thought so. You have that look about you, dorogaya. The same look your grandfather had when he was hiding something important from me." She leaned forward conspiratorially. "So, tell me—what is it that has put that glow in your eyes?"

Taking a deep breath, Mishka met her grandmother's gaze. "I've met someone, Baba."

Sofia's eyebrows rose slightly, but her expression remained encouraging. "Have you now? And this someone—they are special?"

"Very special." Mishka's voice grew stronger, more confident. "This person is—"

"A woman?" Sofia interrupted gently.

Mishka blinked in surprise. "You know then, Baba?"

Sofia laughed, a rich sound that filled the room. "That you're inclined toward women? Of course I do, child. I've known for a long time. A grandmother sees these things, especially when she loves someone as much as I love you."

Relief flooded through Mishka's chest. "I was so afraid you'd be disappointed, or—"

"Disappointed?" Sofia's voice sharpened. "Never. You are exactly who you are meant to be, Mishka. The only thing that would disappoint me is if you tried to be someone else to please others."

"She's..." Mishka struggled to find the right words. "She's the person I've been waiting for my whole life, Baba. I never understood what people meant when they talked about finding their other half, but now I do."

Sofia's expression grew thoughtful, almost wistful. "Ah, yes. I remember that feeling." She stood slowly, moving to the window that overlooked her private garden. "You know, for many years, I had a very close friend. Katarina. We met at the opera—she was a widow, lonely like I was."

Mishka watched her grandmother's reflection in the glass, seeing a vulnerability she rarely revealed.

Dangerous Liaisons

"We were... very close," Sofia continued quietly. "Closer than friends, if you understand my meaning. But I had no choice about marriage when I was young. That is how it was in my day—families arranged these things, and women did what was expected of them."

She turned back to face Mishka, her eyes bright with memory. "But we managed, Katarina and I. You have to be smart about how you operate in this world. We were discreet and did what we wanted anyway. Once I had provided your grandfather with an heir—your father—he left me alone to live as I chose. You have to be clever if you want to get your own way."

The revelation hung in the air between them, recontextualizing everything Mishka thought she knew about her grandmother's life. "Baba, I had no idea..."

"Of course you didn't. We were careful, as we had to be. But those were some of the happiest years of my life." Sofia returned to her chair, her voice becoming practical again. "The difference is, you have choices I never had. You can build the life you want from the beginning."

"Can I though?" The frustration Mishka had been carrying for months suddenly burst forth. "You're smart, Baba. You know I'm smart too. All the women in our family are. I could run this business—I know I could—but I don't have an appendage dangling between my legs."

Sofia's eyebrows shot up at her granddaughter's crude phrasing, but she didn't interrupt.

"Nikolai will be made CEO regardless of whether he can manage it well. It doesn't matter that I have better instincts, better education, better relationships with our partners. It doesn't matter that I understand this industry better than he ever will."

"You're frustrated with your position in the company," Sofia observed calmly.

"I'm furious!" Mishka stood abruptly, pacing to the window. "I watch him stumble through meetings, miss obvious opportunities, make decisions based on ego instead of strategy. And everyone just nods and smiles because he's the heir apparent."

Sofia watched her granddaughter's agitation with the patience of someone who had lived through decades of similar struggles. "True, your brother does not have the spine you have," she said finally. "But he will learn. He has to. This is his birthright."

"What if he doesn't want it?"

The question seemed to surprise Sofia. "Do you seriously think he has a choice?"

"No," Mishka admitted, turning back from the window. "But I do. I'm not going to hang around playing second fiddle forever, Baba. I have my own plans, my own dreams. And now I have someone I want to build something with."

Sofia studied her granddaughter for a long moment, seeing the determination that reminded her so much of herself at that age. "This woman—she shares your ambitions?"

"She understands them. We're talking about starting our own venture. Something that would be ours, where we could make decisions based on merit instead of tradition."

"And leave the family business behind?"

Dangerous Liaisons

The question hung heavy in the air. Mishka sank back into her chair, suddenly feeling the weight of what she was contemplating. "I don't know. Maybe. Is that terrible of me?"

Sofia was quiet for a long time, her fingers drumming thoughtfully against her desk. When she finally spoke, her voice was measured, careful.

"When I was your age, I thought I had no choices. I believed that duty to family meant sacrificing my own happiness, my own dreams. It took me many years to learn that sometimes the best way to serve your family is to be true to yourself."

She leaned forward, fixing Mishka with that penetrating stare again. "But be very careful. The path you're considering—it will change everything. For you, for this woman you love, for all of us. Make sure it's what you really want, not just what you think you want because you're angry."

"I am angry," Mishka admitted. "But it's more than that. I'm tired of waiting for permission to live my life. Tired of pretending that what I want doesn't matter."

Sofia nodded slowly. "Then perhaps it's time you stopped waiting for permission and started taking what you need." Her smile was sharp, predatory. "After all, you are my granddaughter. And I did not raise you to be anyone's second choice."

Sofia's sharp smile faded, replaced by something more serious—an almost imperceptible shadow crossing her features. She reached for the teacup again, but this time didn't sip, merely held it between her fingers, her gaze focused not on Mishka, but on the delicate swirl of steam rising from the rim.

"There is something else I must say, and you will not like it," she said finally, her voice quieter now, tempered by something close to sadness. "You are brave, Mishenka, and bold. And I admire that more than you know. But the world—our world—is not always kind to brave women. Especially not when they love other women."

Mishka straightened in her seat, brows knitting. "But times have changed. It's not like it was in your day."

"Some things have changed. Many things have not," Sofia replied, setting the cup down with a soft clink. "You move in elite circles—moneyed circles. Power, old money, old loyalties. These people may smile, but they will whisper. Not all of them, but enough. Some will try to shut doors quietly, so you do not hear them close."

Mishka's jaw tightened. "Let them whisper."

"Oh, they will. And it will not just be whispers. It will be judgment disguised as concern. It will be invitations that never arrive. Opportunities that vanish without explanation. Backroom deals made without your name on the list." Sofia leaned in slightly. "There are those within our own community—our own extended family—who will not approve. They will speak of tradition. Of 'what is natural.' Of legacy and shame. Some of them already question your role in the company. This will only feed their fire."

"I don't care what they think," Mishka said, though the defiance in her voice didn't quite hide the sting in her chest.

Dangerous Liaisons

"Maybe you don't now. But you might, when it begins to cost you. When investors grow cold. When partners hesitate. When your name becomes... complicated."

Silence bloomed between them.

Sofia softened then, her hand reaching out across the desk. She took Mishka's fingers in her own, the strength in her grip belying her age. "I don't say this to scare you. Only to prepare you. You must go in with your eyes open. Loving a woman, building a life with her—it will be a beautiful thing, yes. But do not expect the world to celebrate it."

Mishka looked down at their joined hands, her voice barely above a whisper. "You said I have choices you never did."

"You do. But choices come with consequences. I made mine, and I lived with them. Some cost me dearly. You must decide what you are willing to risk. And for whom."

For a long moment, neither spoke. Then Mishka nodded slowly. "Allegra is worth the risk."

Sofia smiled again, but this time there was steel beneath it. "Then fight for her. But do it with your head as much as your heart. Be strategic. Be unshakable. You are not a naïve girl in love—you are a woman with a future to build. Protect it."

"I will," Mishka said, her voice steady now. "And Baba... thank you. For warning me. For telling me the truth."

Sofia's eyes glinted with something fierce and proud. "Always, dorogaya. You are my legacy, and my hope. I would never lie to you—only sharpen your blade before you go to war."

She released Mishka's hand and stood with effort, her fingers brushing invisible dust from the sleeve of her silk blouse. "Now go. Make your plans. Love boldly. Just remember—every empire worth building comes at a cost. Choose the price you're willing to pay."

Mishka stood too, heart pounding with both fear and determination. She bent to kiss her grandmother's cheek again, this time lingering just a little longer. "I'll make you proud."

Sofia smiled, but there was a flicker of something unreadable in her gaze—regret, perhaps, or nostalgia. "You already have."

***

Later that evening, the soft hum of the boat's engine was the only sound beneath the lapping of water against the hull. Mishka stood barefoot on the deck, a blanket draped over her shoulders, staring out at the scattered lights of the harbor. Behind her, the warm glow from the salon cast elongated shadows through the glass doors. They had taken the boat out on the water, leaving the dramas of the day on shore.

She didn't turn when she heard the soft creak of the floorboards. She knew Allegra's footsteps by now—the unhurried, confident cadence of a woman used to owning whatever room she walked into.

"You've been quiet since you got back," Allegra said, stepping up beside her.

Mishka nodded, her gaze fixed on the lights in the distance. "I saw my grandmother."

Dangerous Liaisons

"And?" Allegra's voice was calm, but she reached out and slipped her hand into Mishka's, lacing their fingers together.

"She knows about us. Knew, apparently, before I ever said a word."

"That doesn't surprise me."

"She wasn't angry," Mishka said. "In fact, she was... supportive. But she also warned me."

Allegra turned toward her. "About what?"

"That there will be backlash. From inside the family. From the wider community. Business associates. There are still people—powerful people—who won't look kindly on me being with you. Not because of *you*, but because you're a woman. Because we're not the right kind of couple to parade at donor dinners or industry galas."

Allegra was quiet for a beat. "Do *you* care?"

"No. Not enough to walk away. But I care about what it might cost us. I care about being shut out of opportunities. I care about the way people will look at you. At *us*." Mishka's voice caught. "I don't want to lose anything. But I also don't want to hide."

"You won't have to," Allegra said gently. "Not with me."

Mishka turned to her then, eyes searching. "You know this isn't going to be easy."

Allegra nodded. "Good things rarely are."

Mishka let out a shaky breath. "Then we'll be strong. Together."

Allegra brought their joined hands to her lips and kissed Mishka's knuckles. "You don't have to do this alone. Whatever comes, we'll face it side by side."

Mishka pulled her in, wrapping her arms around Allegra's waist, burying her face against her neck. For a long moment they stood there, two silhouettes against the harbor lights, hearts aligned even as storm clouds gathered on the horizon.

But then Mishka pulled back slightly, a new tension creeping into her voice.

"There's something else," she said.

Allegra's brow furrowed. "What is it?"

"Has anyone asked questions about Tony?"

Allegra's expression darkened. "No. Not directly. There may have been whispers. You?"

"Nothing yet. But I keep thinking about the dock. Where he boarded the boat that night."

Allegra stiffened. "CCTV?"

Mishka nodded. "If there was a camera nearby—if it was working—there might be footage of him getting on board. And no footage of him getting off."

"That's... unlikely. The marina's private. Minimal surveillance, if any."

"I'll check. We need to be sure," Mishka said, her voice taut. "Because if there *is* footage, and someone's looking... it's enough to start questions we're not ready to answer."

Allegra's mouth was a firm line. "I'll call in a favour. Quietly. We'll find out."

Mishka nodded. "Thank you."

They fell silent again, the weight of the moment settling around them like fog. Allegra wrapped her arms tighter around Mishka, anchoring them both.

"We'll protect what we've built," she said softly. "No matter what it takes."

Mishka closed her eyes and leaned into her. "I believe you."

Chapter 13

THE INTRODUCTION TO Sofia Volkov had gone better than Allegra could have hoped. The elderly matriarch had received her with warmth and shrewd assessment, in a sitting room that seemed untouched by time—ivory silk drapes, an antique crystal chandelier, and polished wood gleaming beneath oriental rugs. Sofia sat like a queen in her high-backed chair, every movement deliberate, every glance sharpened with quiet power. Her eyes, pale grey and shrewd, studied Allegra like a chess opponent assessing an opening move. Allegra had dressed with care—a tailored cream blouse, understated jewellery, nothing too bold—but she still felt exposed under Sofia's scrutiny.

"So," Sofia said, her voice accented, rich with control, "you are the daughter. *La figlia Castelli*. I have heard a great deal about you."

"And I've heard even more about you," Allegra replied, forcing a polite smile. "It's an honour to meet you."

Sofia gave a gracious nod, her gaze narrowing slightly, as if trying to see past the words. "You are calm. Poised. Too calm for a woman in love, perhaps?"

Dangerous Liaisons

Allegra blinked.

Sofia chuckled softly. "Ah. There it is—the flicker. Don't worry, I do not ask to embarrass you. I ask because I have eyes. And my granddaughter—she has changed. Her voice when she speaks of you is... softer. More dangerous."

Allegra dared a question. "Dangerous?"

"Because love is dangerous. Especially when it crosses lines our families pretend no longer exist."

Before Allegra could respond, Mishka entered carrying a tray of tea and delicate pastries. She set it down with a practiced ease and kissed her grandmother's cheek.

"Baba, I hope you're being kind."

"I'm always kind," Sofia said with a smile that made both younger women exchange a knowing look.

When Mishka stepped out briefly to retrieve a folder, Sofia leaned in, conspiratorially.

"She has spoken to me about you," she said, voice low. "And now I see why."

Allegra felt warmth rise to her cheeks. "That means a great deal."

Sofia studied her a beat longer, then leaned back. "You are strong. But strength will not shield you from everything. There will be people who do not approve of this bond. Even now, even here. And some will not whisper—they will act."

Allegra met her gaze. "We're prepared."

"No one is ever truly prepared. Not for the ways power resists change. Not for betrayal dressed in family colours." Her fingers tapped once on the armrest. "But if you are willing to bleed for each other... then perhaps you stand a chance."

Before Allegra could answer, Mishka returned, and the conversation pivoted to business. But Sofia's words stayed with her, but that had been three weeks ago, before everything started unravelling.

The call came on a Tuesday morning while Allegra was reviewing contracts in her office. Her father's voice was tight with barely controlled anger.

"The *Harbour Light* project meeting is postponed indefinitely," Gianni announced without preamble.

"What? Papa, why?"

"That bastard Mikhail thinks he can dictate terms to me. Thinks because his hotels have fancy lobbies, he can treat the Castellis like junior partners." The fury in her father's voice made Allegra's stomach clench. "We're done with them. Find us another investment opportunity."

"But the contracts are nearly finalized—"

"I said we're done, Allegra. The Volkovs can build their monument to excess without us."

The line went dead, leaving Allegra staring at her phone in horror. Whatever business disagreement had erupted between their fathers, it would make any continued contact with Mishka nearly impossible. Family loyalty would demand they stay on their respective sides of the divide.

Her hands shook as she called Mishka's private number.

"I heard," Mishka said before Allegra could speak. "My father is furious. Something about territorial rights for the harbor development."

"Can we fix this?"

Dangerous Liaisons

"Not quickly. You know how these men are when their pride is involved." Mishka's voice was heavy with frustration. "We need to be careful, Allegra. Very careful."

***

The parking garage beneath Allegra's apartment building felt secure, private. She'd chosen the space deliberately—far from prying eyes, with multiple exit routes. But as she walked toward her car three days after the consortium collapsed, every shadow seemed to hold threat.

Riccardo stepped out from behind a concrete pillar, his presence so unexpected that Allegra nearly dropped her keys.

"Hello, Allegra. We need to talk."

"Jesus, Riccardo! You scared me to death." Her heart hammered against her ribs as she tried to project calm authority. "What are you doing here?"

"Waiting for you. We have some unfinished business."

Something in his tone made her skin crawl. Riccardo looked different—thinner, with dark circles under his eyes and a desperate edge that hadn't been there before. The confident swagger was gone, replaced by something more dangerous.

"If this is about the engagement—"

"It's about Tony Marcelli." Riccardo moved closer, close enough that she could smell whiskey on his breath despite the early hour. "Funny thing about Tony. He just disappeared. Poof. Gone without a trace."

Allegra forced herself to remain still, though every instinct screamed at her to run. "I wouldn't know anything about that."

"Wouldn't you?" Riccardo's smile was cold, calculating. "See, Tony was working for me. Following you, taking pictures, gathering information. Very interesting information, as it turns out."

Her blood turned to ice, but outwardly she maintained her composure. She couldn't let him see she was terrified. "I don't know what you're talking about."

"The Russian woman. Mishka Volkov." Riccardo pulled out his phone, swiping to a photograph that made Allegra's world tilt sideways. It showed her and Mishka on the hotel balcony, locked in an intimate embrace. "Tony was very thorough in his surveillance. Right up until he vanished."

The concrete walls of the garage seemed to close in around her. "That doesn't prove anything."

"Doesn't it? Tony had hours of footage, Allegra. Audio recordings of very private conversations. All stored in a cloud account that I now have access to." Riccardo's voice dropped to a whisper. "The question is, what happened to Tony? And what might a desperate woman do to protect her secrets?"

"You're fishing," Allegra said, but her voice sounded hollow even to her own ears.

"Am I? Let me paint you a picture. Tony calls you, threatens to expose your little lesbian affair. You panic. Maybe you arrange to meet him somewhere private. Maybe things get out of hand." Riccardo stepped even closer, his breath hot against her ear. "Maybe accidents happen when people are desperate."

"That's insane. You're hallucinating"

Dangerous Liaisons

"Is it? Because here's what I think happened—Tony was blackmailing you, and now he's gone. Your family, your father's business, your precious reputation... all of it would be destroyed if certain photographs became public. That's a hell of a motive."

Allegra's mind raced, looking for escape routes, for options. He had no proof. He couldn't have. Surely there wasn't any. Surreptitiously, she clutched her keys in her hand, ready to use as a makeshift weapon.

"What do you want?"

"Smart girl. I want my life back, Allegra. You destroyed my engagement prospects, ruined my standing with my father. Left me with debts I can't pay and enemies I can't avoid." His smile was vicious. "So, here's the deal. You're going to convince your father to reconsider our marriage arrangement. You're going to be the perfect, dutiful daughter and marry me like a good Italian girl should."

"Never."

"Oh, I think you will. Because the alternative is that these photos find their way to your father. To the newspapers. To everyone who matters in your carefully constructed little world." Riccardo held up his phone, thumb hovering over the screen. "I wonder what Gianni Castelli will think when he learns his precious daughter prefers pussy to—"

The slap echoed through the garage like a gunshot. Riccardo's head snapped to the side, a red handprint blooming across his cheek.

"You piece of shit," Allegra snarled, her composure finally cracking. "You think you can—"

"I think I can do whatever I want," Riccardo said, touching his cheek with something like admiration. "Because I hold all the cards now."

"Not all of them."

The new voice came from behind Riccardo, cool and controlled. Mishka stepped into the circle of light, her presence immediately shifting the dynamic in the garage. She was dressed in dark clothing, with a cap covering her hair.

Riccardo spun around, his confidence wavering for the first time. "Who the hell—"

"Mishka Volkov," she said smoothly, extending her hand as if they were meeting at a cocktail party and hadn't met before. "I believe you've been looking at unauthorized photographs of me."

Riccardo's eyes darted between the two women, calculating odds. "The Russian bitch. This is perfect—both of you here for the grand finale."

"Such charming language," Mishka observed. "I can see why Allegra found you so irresistible."

"This doesn't change anything," Riccardo said, but uncertainty crept into his voice. "I still have the photos, the recordings—"

"Do you?" Mishka's smile was arctic. "Because I find that hard to believe, given that Tony Ricci never had any such materials to begin with."

"Bullshit. He showed me—"

"He showed you fabricated evidence. Photoshopped images designed to convince you that he had something valuable to sell." Mishka's voice was patient, almost pitying.

Dangerous Liaisons

"Poor Tony. He was always more ambitious than talented. He couldn't even successfully follow a target. He stood out like dog's balls. Did you really think he could successfully blackmail two families like ours?"

Riccardo's face went pale. "You're lying."

"Am I? Then why don't you show us these damning photographs? Let's see the quality of Tony's surveillance work."

With shaking hands, Riccardo fumbled with his phone, swiping through files. His expression grew increasingly frantic as he searched.

"They were here. They were right here!"

"Were they? Or did Tony convince you that blurry, distant shots of two women having a business conversation were something more incriminating than they actually were?"

Allegra watched the exchange with growing amazement. Mishka was systematically dismantling Riccardo's confidence, turning his certainty into doubt.

"Even if the photos exist," Mishka continued relentlessly, "what exactly do they prove? That two businesswomen met to discuss a hotel development? That they shared a professional dinner? How scandalous."

"I heard the audio—"

"Did you? Or did you hear what Tony wanted you to hear? What he thought you'd pay for?" Mishka stepped closer to Riccardo, her voice dropping to a dangerous whisper. "You see, Riccardo, the problem with dealing with amateurs is that they make amateur mistakes. And you've made the biggest mistake of all."

"What mistake?"

"You've threatened us. Both of us. Our families take threats very seriously. You think the Mafia is something to be feared? You'd be right, but it's nothing to what the Russian bratva would do to you."

The colour drained completely from Riccardo's face as the implications sank in. He was trapped between two powerful families, having made enemies of both with his clumsy blackmail attempt.

"This isn't over," he said, but the words lacked conviction.

"Yes," Mishka said calmly, "it is. You're going to delete whatever files you think you have. You're going to stop following Allegra, stop making threats, and disappear from our lives completely. Because if you don't..."

She let the sentence hang unfinished, more threatening in its implication than any explicit threat could have been.

Riccardo looked between them one more time, his desperate gambit crumbling around him. Without another word, he turned and fled toward the garage exit, his footsteps echoing off the concrete walls.

Allegra leaned against her car, legs suddenly unsteady. "How did you know to come here?"

"I've been watching you since the consortium fell apart. I was worried Riccardo might try something desperate." Mishka moved to her side, close enough to offer comfort without being obvious about it. "Are you all right?"

"I think so. But Mishka, what if he really does have photos? What if—"

Dangerous Liaisons

"He doesn't. Tony never had anything useful, I made sure of that and all his equipment is currently rather wet." Mishka's voice was matter-of-fact, chilling in its calm certainty. "I also have connections who were able to hack his account—for a fee."

Allegra stared at her, understanding dawning. "You suspected. You suspected this whole time that Riccardo might come after us."

"I knew he was desperate. Desperate people do unpredictable things." Mishka's hand found hers, squeezing gently. "But he's finished now. His credibility is shot, his family's patience is exhausted, and he's made enemies he can't afford to have."

"And Tony?"

Mishka's expression didn't change. "Tony made his choices. We made ours."

The weight of their shared secret settled between them again, binding them together in ways that went beyond love. They had protected each other, protected their future, and emerged stronger for it.

But as they stood in the shadows of the parking garage, Allegra couldn't shake the feeling that they had crossed another line they could never uncross. The game they were playing had stakes higher than she'd ever imagined, and the cost of losing was more than either of them could bear.

"What happens now?" she asked quietly.

"Now we go home," Mishka said. "Separately, carefully. And we wait to see what our fathers decide about the future."

"And us?"

Mishka's smile was fierce, determined. "We survive. Whatever it takes, we survive."

Chapter 14

RICCARDO ROSSINI SAT in the back booth of Torrino's, a dive bar three blocks from the docks, nursing his fourth whiskey of the evening. The ice had long since melted, leaving the amber liquid warm and bitter on his tongue. Around him, the bar hummed with the low conversation of dock workers and small-time criminals—his people now, he supposed. The expensive suits and exclusive clubs were behind him.

His phone buzzed against the scarred wooden table. Another creditor, another threat, another door slamming shut. He'd burned through his trust fund, maxed out every credit line, and his father had made it crystal clear that the family name would no longer protect him from his own stupidity.

"Stupid bitch," he muttered into his glass, the words slurring slightly. "Both of them."

"Talking to yourself now, Riccardo? That's not a good sign."

He looked up to find Danny Torrino sliding into the booth across from him. Danny was younger than Riccardo by five years, but the streets had aged him prematurely. His face bore the scars of too many fights, and his knuckles were permanently swollen from breaking too many bones.

"Danny." Riccardo straightened slightly, trying to project sobriety. "What brings you to this shithole?"

"It's my uncle's bar, asshole. I'm here most nights." Danny signalled the bartender for two fresh drinks. "But tonight, I'm here because I heard you might have a proposition for me."

Riccardo's pulse quickened. Danny Torrino ran a crew of muscle-for-hire, guys who'd break legs for the right price and ask no questions. Exactly what Riccardo needed.

"Depends. You still in the... problem-solving business?"

"I solve all kinds of problems." Danny's smile was cold. "Question is, what's your problem worth to you?"

Riccardo leaned forward, lowering his voice despite the bar's din. "There's a woman. Allegra Castelli. She's made my life difficult, and I want to return the favour."

"Castelli?" Danny's eyebrows shot up. "As in Gianni Castelli? You want me to fuck with the Mafia?"

"Not hurt her," Riccardo said quickly. "Just... hold her for a while. Make her father sweat. Make her understand that actions have consequences."

Danny leaned back, studying Riccardo with new interest. "You're talking about kidnapping."

"I'm talking about a business transaction. Her father or business connections will pay anything to get her back safely. We split the ransom, everybody wins."

"Except the girl."

Riccardo's expression hardened. "She'll be fine. A little scared, maybe, but fine. Consider it a learning experience."

Dangerous Liaisons

Danny was quiet for a long moment, swirling the whiskey in his glass. When he spoke again, his voice was businesslike. "What kind of money are we talking?"

"Millions. Her father's worth fifty million, easy. Even if we only ask for one or two..."

"That's a lot of heat for a kidnapping."

"That's a lot of money for a few days' work." Riccardo reached into his jacket and pulled out a thick envelope. "There's five grand in there. A down payment. Think about it, Danny. When's the last time you made that kind of score?"

Danny took the envelope, hefting its weight. Riccardo had his attention now.

"I'd need two other guys. Professionals."

"Whatever you need."

"And we do this clean. No one gets hurt if they cooperate."

"Absolutely."

Danny was quiet again, then nodded slowly. "All right, Riccardo. But we do this my way. You don't get to call the shots just because you're paying."

Riccardo's smile was vicious. "Deal. But I want to be there when we take her. I want to see her face when she realizes she's not untouchable."

"Fine by me. You got any idea about her routine? Where she goes, when she's vulnerable?"

Riccardo pulled out his phone, scrolling through the photos he'd been taking over the past week. "She's been meeting with someone regularly. Dinner dates, drinks. I think she might have a new relationship."

He showed Danny a grainy photo of Allegra walking into an upscale restaurant with a woman Danny didn't recognize.

"Who's the woman?"

"Doesn't matter. But they meet at least twice a week, always at the same kinds of places. Expensive, trendy. Places where rich people feel safe."

Danny studied the photo more carefully. "We'll need to watch her for a few more days, learn the pattern. But yeah, this could work."

They spent the next hour planning, their voices low and conspiratorial. By the time they parted ways, Riccardo felt more alive than he had in weeks. Finally, finally, he would get his revenge.

***

Three days later, Allegra sat across from Mishka at Meridian, a new fusion restaurant that had quickly become one of the city's most sought-after reservations. The lighting was warm and intimate, casting golden shadows across the table between them. Despite everything that had happened with their families, these stolen moments felt precious.

"The sea bass is incredible," Mishka said, cutting another delicate piece. "Though I have to admit, I'm distracted."

"By what?" Allegra asked, though she suspected she knew the answer.

"By you. By this whole impossible situation." Mishka's voice dropped lower. "My father asked me again today if I'd been in contact with any Castellis."

"What did you tell him?"

Dangerous Liaisons

"I said that business was business, but blood was blood." Mishka's smile was rueful. "He seemed satisfied with that non-answer."

"And if he found out the truth?"

"He'd probably lock me in my room until I came to my senses." Mishka reached across the table, her fingers brushing against Allegra's. "What about your father?"

"He'd kill me. Or marry me off to the first available Italian boy he could find." Allegra turned her hand palm up, letting their fingers intertwine briefly. "Maybe both."

They were interrupted by the waiter bringing dessert—a shared chocolate soufflé that they'd ordered more for the excuse to lean closer together than from actual hunger. As Mishka lifted a spoonful to her lips, Allegra felt a familiar warmth spread through her chest. How had she gotten so lucky?

"I've been thinking," Mishka said quietly. "About what my grandmother said. About survival."

"What about it?"

"Maybe we need to stop being so careful. We should take control of the situation instead of letting our fathers dictate our lives."

Allegra felt her pulse quicken. "What are you suggesting?"

"I'm suggesting that if they won't let us build bridges, maybe we need to force their hands. Show them that their feud is costing them more than their pride is worth. Aside from that, I want to start working on The Matilda. That's a project that won't wait."

Before Allegra could respond, Mishka's phone buzzed against the table. She glanced at it and frowned.

"Work emergency. I need to take this, but it'll just be a minute."

"Of course. I'll get the check."

Mishka squeezed her hand before stepping outside to take the call. Allegra watched her go, admiring the confident way she moved through the restaurant. Other diners' eyes followed her too—Mishka had that kind of presence that demanded attention.

The waiter brought the check, and as Allegra swiped her credit card, she had an uncomfortable feeling of being observed. Looking up, she saw a man at the bar watching her intently. He was young, maybe mid-twenties, with the kind of hard edges that spoke of a rough life. When their eyes met, he looked away quickly, but not before she caught something calculating in his expression.

A chill ran down her spine. Something felt wrong. What was he doing there? He didn't belong. She finished signing and gathered her purse, suddenly eager to rejoin Mishka outside. As she stood, the man from the bar was already moving toward the exit. He reached the door just as she did, holding it open with what might have been courtesy if not for the way his eyes lingered on her face.

"Thank you," she said politely, stepping past him onto the sidewalk.

Mishka was still on her phone a few feet away, speaking in rapid Russian. The man from the bar lingered nearby, lighting a cigarette with hands that seemed too steady.

"Ready?" Mishka asked, ending her call.

"More than ready. Let's go."

They walked toward where their cars were parked in a lot two blocks away. The evening air was crisp, and the streets were busy with late diners and bar hoppers. Normal city sounds, normal city life. But Allegra couldn't shake the feeling that they were being watched.

"Everything all right?" Mishka asked, noticing her tension.

"I'm probably being paranoid, but there was a man at the restaurant. He was watching me."

Mishka's expression immediately sharpened. "What did he look like?"

"Young, dark hair, scar on his left cheek. He held the door for me when we left, but something about him felt off."

Mishka glanced around casually, her gaze sweeping the street behind them. "I don't see anyone matching that description now."

"Like I said, probably just paranoia."

But as they reached Mishka's car, Allegra's anxiety spiked again. The parking lot was poorly lit, with deep shadows between the vehicles. Perfect for someone who wanted to stay hidden.

"Maybe I should drive you home tonight," Mishka said, reading her mood. "We can get your car tomorrow."

"No, it's fine. I'm just being—"

The attack came from between two SUVs parked near Allegra's car. Two men rushed them from the shadows, moving with practiced coordination. The first man—not the one from the restaurant, but older, heavier—grabbed Allegra from behind, clamping a hand over her mouth before she could scream.

Mishka spun toward her attacker, but the second man was ready. He caught her wrist as she reached for her phone, twisting her arm behind her back.

"Don't make this difficult," he said quietly. "We just want the girl."

Allegra struggled against the arm around her throat, her heart hammering with pure terror. Over the man's shoulder, she could see Mishka's face, contorted with fury and fear.

"Let her go," Mishka said, her voice deadly calm despite the gun now pressed against her ribs. "You have no idea what you're starting."

"We know exactly what we're starting," the gunman replied. "And we know exactly how it's going to end."

A van pulled up to the entrance of the lot, its engine running. The back doors swung open, revealing a third man waiting inside.

"Time to go," the man holding Allegra said. He pressed something that smelled sickeningly sweet against her nose and mouth. Chloroform, she realized with growing panic. She tried to hold her breath, but her lungs were already burning from the struggle.

"Allegra!" Mishka's voice seemed to come from very far away. "Don't—"

The world tilted sideways, colours bleeding into each other like watercolours in rain. The last thing Allegra saw

Dangerous Liaisons

before consciousness slipped away was Mishka fighting against her captors, her face a mask of rage and desperation.

Then everything went dark.

***

Mishka watched in horror as they dragged Allegra's unconscious form toward the van. The man holding her was professional, efficient—he'd done this before. The van's license plate was obscured, and the men were dressed in dark clothing that would make them impossible to identify in security footage.

"Let me go," she said to the man still holding her. "I won't follow you."

"Smart girl. But just to be sure..."

The blow came from behind, a sap to the base of her skull that sent stars exploding across her vision. She collapsed to her knees, fighting to stay conscious as the van doors slammed shut and the vehicle sped away into the night.

By the time her head cleared enough to stand, they were long gone.

Mishka pulled out her phone with shaking hands, her mind racing through options. Call the police? They'd ask too many questions, involve too many people. This felt personal, targeted. Someone who knew Allegra's routine, knew about their relationship.

Riccardo.

The name came to her with cold certainty. He'd been desperate enough to try blackmail; kidnapping wasn't that much of a leap. And he'd have the connections to hire professional muscle.

The number she wanted was on speed dial. It rang twice before he answered.

"Enrico Castelli."

"Rico, I need your help. Your cousin Allegra's been taken."

There was a pause, then Enrico's voice sharpened with concern. "Taken? What happened?"

"Three men, professional job. They grabbed her from a restaurant parking lot twenty minutes ago. We had dined at the Meridian." Mishka's voice was steady, but held underlying panic. "I think Riccardo Rossini is behind it."

"Riccardo! Are you sure? Are you hurt?"

"I'm fine. But Rico, if they hurt her..." Her voice trailed off, the threat implicit.

"They won't. We'll find her." Enrico's voice was grimly determined. "Where are you now?"

"Still at the scene. I haven't called the police yet."

"Good. Don't. This needs to be handled quietly." Enrico was already moving; she could hear him grabbing keys, opening doors. "I'm on my way. Don't go anywhere alone, don't trust anyone. Allegra told me he was hassling her, but if this is Riccardo, he's more desperate than we thought."

"Rico," Mishka said, her voice barely above a whisper. "If something happens to her because of me, because of what we are to each other..."

"Nothing's going to happen to her. We'll bring her home."

As Mishka ended the call and stared at the empty parking lot where Allegra had been taken, she couldn't shake the feeling that they were already too late.

***

Allegra woke to the sound of water dripping somewhere in the darkness. Her head throbbed, and the taste of chloroform lingered bitter on her tongue. She tried to move and discovered her hands were zip-tied behind her back, secured to what felt like a metal chair.

"She's awake."

The voice came from somewhere to her left, male and unfamiliar. She tried to turn toward it, but a blindfold blocked her vision completely.

"Good. Boss wants to talk to her."

Footsteps approached, and Allegra forced herself to breathe slowly, fighting down the panic that threatened to overwhelm her. Think, she told herself. Listen. Learn everything you can.

The air smelled of motor oil and rust, with an underlying dampness that suggested they were near water. A warehouse, maybe, or a garage. The acoustics were large and echoing, confirming her guess about the space.

"Well, well. The princess awakens."

This voice she recognized, even though it was trying to sound different—deeper, more controlled. Riccardo. Her blood ran cold, but she kept her expression neutral.

"I don't know who you are or what you want," she said, proud that her voice didn't shake. "But my father will pay whatever ransom you're asking. You don't need to hurt me."

"Oh, this isn't about money, princess. Well, not entirely." Riccardo moved closer; she could smell his cologne, that expensive scent he'd always worn. "This is about respect. About consequences."

He was standing directly in front of her now, close enough that she could feel his breath on her face. Every instinct screamed at her to recoil, but she forced herself to remain still.

"I don't understand."

"Of course you don't. You've never had to face consequences for your actions, have you? Never had to pay for the lives you've destroyed."

Riccardo's hand touched her cheek, a gentle caress that made her skin crawl. She jerked away instinctively.

"Don't touch me."

"I'll touch you however and wherever I want." His voice hardened, the mask and pretence slipping. "You're not in control anymore, Allegra. For the first time in your privileged life, someone else is calling the shots."

"What do you want?"

"I want my life back. I want my father's respect back. I want the money and the connections and the future that you took from me." Riccardo's voice was rising, becoming more unstable. He didn't even try to hide his identity. "And I want you to understand what it feels like to lose everything."

Dangerous Liaisons

Allegra's mind raced. Riccardo was clearly unhinged, operating on pure rage and desperation. That made him unpredictable, dangerous. But it also made him sloppy.

"My father will notice I'm missing," she said. "He'll come looking for me."

"Will he? Or will he assume you've run off with your Russian whore?"

"I don't know what you're talking about."

Riccardo's laugh was harsh. "Please. I've been watching you for weeks. Cozy dinners, intimate conversations, the way you look at each other like you're the only two people in the world."

Allegra's throat tightened with fear. Riccardo had the power to destroy both their families. The kidnapping might just be the beginning.

"So, here's what's going to happen," Riccardo continued. "You're going to call your father. You're going to tell him that you've been having second thoughts about our engagement. That you realize you made a mistake, and you want to make things right."

"I'll never—"

"Oh, you will. Because I know where all the bodies are buried, Allegra." Riccardo's voice dropped to a whisper that somehow felt more menacing than his earlier shouting. "Your father's role in various... underhand activities. The deals, the arrangements, the favours, the people who've disappeared. All of it."

Allegra's blood ran cold. She could hear the satisfaction in his voice—the cold satisfaction of a man holding all the cards.

"If I tell all," Riccardo continued, circling her slowly, "it won't just be the long arm of the law that comes knocking. The brothers in Sydney will be very interested to hear about Gianni's business practices. Very interested indeed."

He paused, letting the words sink in. "Not only will your family lose everything—every asset seized by the authorities as proceeds of crime—but your father... well, retribution from the brothers can be swift and without mercy. Even your life could be under threat."

Allegra's mind raced. She knew he was telling the truth. There had always been things about her father's business she didn't ask about, conversations that stopped when she entered the room. Papa had wanted to shield her from what he called "men's business," wanted her to have the education and sophistication he'd never had. His protection had become her blindness.

"You're lying," she whispered, but even she could hear the uncertainty in her voice.

Riccardo moved away, his footsteps echoing in the large space. When he spoke again, his voice came from farther away, more casual, as if discussing the weather.

"Think about it, Allegra. Think about what matters more—your little Russian romance, or keeping your father alive. Because make no mistake, if the Sydney families learn what I know, Gianni won't survive the week."

Dangerous Liaisons

Allegra's throat constricted. She needed time to think, to find another way out of this nightmare. "I... I need to process this. You can't expect me to just—"

"Oh, but I can." Riccardo's footsteps returned, closer now. "But I'm not unreasonable. You have until tomorrow night to make the call. After that..." He let the threat hang in the air.

Allegra's mind spun through possibilities, each one more impossible than the last. There had to be a way out of this dilemma. There had to be. She heard him talking to someone else in low tones, but couldn't make out the words. This was her chance to learn more about her surroundings, to find some advantage.

The chair she was tied to felt industrial, heavy. The floor beneath her feet was concrete, cold and slightly damp. When she shifted her weight, she could hear the chair legs scraping against what sounded like grit and debris. Definitely a warehouse or storage facility. Perhaps somewhere on the outskirts of the city, given how long the van ride had felt before she'd lost consciousness completely.

More footsteps approached, lighter this time. A different man.

"How's our guest doing?" This voice was younger, with a rougher edge. One of the kidnappers, probably.

"She's thinking about her options," Riccardo replied. "Give her a few more hours to let reality sink in."

"And if she doesn't cooperate?"

There was a pause that made Allegra's blood freeze.

"Then we move to Plan B," Riccardo said finally. "And trust me, she won't like Plan B nearly as much."

The men moved away again, their conversation fading into indistinct murmurs. Allegra tested the zip ties around her wrists, trying to find any give in the plastic. They were tight, professionally applied. Whoever Riccardo had hired knew what they were doing.

But as she sat in the darkness, one thought kept her from despair. Mishka had seen the attack. She would have called for help by now. And if there was one thing Allegra had learned about the woman she loved, it was that Mishka Volkov never gave up on the people she cared about.

Hold on, she told herself. Just hold on a little longer.

Chapter 15

ENRICO FOUND MISHKA exactly where she'd said she'd be, standing at the edge of the parking lot where Allegra had been taken. She was staring at the spot where the van had been, her expression carved from stone.

"Any word from the kidnappers yet?" he asked without preamble.

"Nothing. But it's Riccardo, I'm sure of it." Mishka turned to face him, and Enrico was struck by the controlled fury in her eyes. "He's finally snapped completely."

"Walk me through what happened."

Mishka recounted the attack in precise detail, her voice steady despite the obvious strain. Enrico listened without interruption, his mind already working through possibilities.

"Professional job," he concluded. "Three men, coordination, a van ready for extraction. Riccardo doesn't have those resources."

"He has money troubles. Desperate people find desperate solutions."

"Or desperate allies." Enrico pulled out his phone. "I'm going to make some calls, see if anyone's heard chatter about a kidnapping job. Riccardo might be orchestrating this, but he's not doing it alone."

"What can I do?"

"Nothing risky. We need to be smart about this." Enrico's expression was grim. "If they're professionals, they'll contact us with demands soon. Until then, we gather information."

As if summoned by his words, Mishka's phone buzzed. Unknown number.

"That's them," she said, her finger hovering over the answer button.

"Put it on speaker," Enrico instructed. "And keep them talking as long as possible."

Mishka answered the call. "Yes?"

"Ms. Antonov." The voice was electronically distorted, unrecognizable. "We have something that belongs to you."

"Where is she? Is she hurt?"

"She's alive. Whether she stays that way depends on how cooperative you are."

Enrico gestured for Mishka to keep the caller engaged while he activated a recording and tracing app on his own phone.

"What do you want?" Mishka asked.

"Five million dollars. Unmarked bills, non-sequential serial numbers. You have forty-eight hours."

"Five million? That's—"

"Pocket change for families like yours. Don't insult my intelligence."

"I need proof she's alive."

There was a pause, then muffled sounds in the background. A moment later, Allegra's voice came through the phone, strained but unmistakably hers.

"Mishka? I'm okay. Don't give them anything. Don't—"

The line went dead.

Enrico checked his tracing app and swore under his breath. "They're using a burner, probably bouncing the signal through multiple towers. But the background noise..." He played back the recording. "Did you hear that? Industrial sounds, maybe machinery running."

"Warehouse district," Mishka said immediately. "Has to be."

"That's a lot of territory to cover. We need to narrow it down." Nikolai was already scrolling through his contacts. "I know someone who might be able to help. I'll put the word out."

***

Twenty minutes later, they sat in a coffee shop downtown across from a man who looked like he'd stepped out of a noir film. Vincent Torrino was Danny's older brother, and while Danny ran muscle, Vincent dealt in information. He had contacts throughout the criminal underworld and a reputation for discretion that made him valuable to people on both sides of the law.

"You're asking me to rat out my own brother," Vincent said, stirring sugar into his espresso with deliberate slowness.

"I'm asking you to prevent a war," Nikolai replied. "Because that's what's going to happen if Allegra Rossini doesn't come home safe. The Castellis will blame the Rossinis, the Volkovs will get involved, and your brother's going to end up in the crossfire."

Vincent considered this, his weathered face impassive. "What makes you think Danny's involved?"

"Riccardo Rossini doesn't have the connections to pull off a professional kidnapping," Mishka said. "But he has access to money through a successful kidnapping, and your brother has a reputation for taking jobs that pay well."

"Hypothetically," Enrico said slowly, "if Danny were involved in something like this, where might he take someone he needed to keep secure?"

Vincent leaned forward. "Hypothetically, there's an old fish processing plant on Pier 47. Been abandoned for years, but the structure's sound. Good acoustics for keeping someone quiet, multiple exits if things go bad." Vincent met their eyes. "Hypothetically."

"Thank you," Mishka said, standing.

"Wait." Vincent caught her arm gently. "If this goes sideways, if people start shooting, my brother's just muscle. He's not the real enemy here."

"Neither is Allegra," Mishka replied. "But someone's going to pay for taking her."

***

"Do we call the police? What about reinforcements?" Mishka's threw out the options as they jumped in the car.

"No police. Not yet. We don't want the family embroiled in any trouble. We'll suss out the situation first. I've brought a

Dangerous Liaisons

bag of tricks with me. You drive, and I'll call the company muscle for back-up. If we wait for them, it might be too late."

Enrico was right. Mishka was relieved to have his support. She gripped the steering wheel tightly, aware that it wasn't just Allegra who was in danger. In pitting themselves against the kidnappers, possibly neither of them would emerge from the warehouse unscathed, if at all.

The fish processing plant squatted on the pier like a diseased tooth, its windows broken and walls streaked with rust. It was after midnight now, and the area was deserted except for the occasional patrol of harbor security. Enrico and Mishka crouched behind a shipping container, studying the building.

"Two guards outside," Enrico whispered, passing her the night binoculars. "Probably more inside."

"How do we get her out without starting a war?"

"Carefully." Enrico checked his weapon, a compact pistol he'd retrieved from his car. "I go in the front, create a distraction and keep them occupied. You take the service entrance on the east side. Find Allegra and if you can do so safely, get her out."

"What about Riccardo?"

Enrico's expression was cold. "Riccardo made his choice when he decided to threaten our family. Whatever happens to him, he brought on himself."

They synchronized their watches and moved into position. The next few minutes would determine whether Allegra came home safe, or whether the fragile peace between their families shattered completely.

Mishka reached the service entrance just as Nikolai's distraction began—a small explosion near the front of the building that sent the guards running toward the sound. She slipped inside through a door that had been left propped open, probably for quick escape routes.

The interior of the plant was a maze of rusted machinery and abandoned workstations. The smell of old fish oil mixed with motor grease made her stomach turn. She moved carefully, using the shadows to mask her approach.

Voices echoed from the main floor—angry, panicked voices. Riccardo's among them.

"What the hell was that?"

"Someone's here. Has to be cops."

"Nobody's supposed to know about this place!"

Mishka followed the sound, keeping low. Through a gap in the machinery, she could see Allegra tied to a chair in the centre of a cleared area. She was blindfolded but alert, her head turning toward the sounds of commotion.

Three men besides Riccardo. Two she didn't recognize, but the third was definitely Danny Torrino. His scarred face was unmistakable, even in the dim light.

Another explosion echoed from the front of the building, closer this time. Nikolai was moving systematically, keeping the guards' focus away from the main area.

"We need to go," Danny said urgently. "Cut our losses and run."

"No!" Riccardo's voice was shrill with panic. "This is my only shot. Without the ransom money, I'm finished."

"You're finished anyway if the cops find us here."

"It's not cops," Riccardo said, realization dawning in his voice. "It's them. The Russians. They found us."

Danny's expression changed, fear replacing annoyance. "Russians? You said this was just about money!"

"The cops wouldn't use explosives. That Volkov woman must have called for back-up. It *is* about money. But they're not going to let us walk away, especially not taking this bitch."

Mishka had heard enough. She needed to act before the situation escalated further. Moving carefully, she worked her way around the perimeter of the cleared area, staying in the shadows cast by the overhead machinery.

Allegra seemed to sense something, her head turning slightly in Mishka's direction. For a moment, their eyes met across the distance—or would have, if not for the blindfold. But there was something in Allegra's posture that suggested she knew help was near.

Mishka reached into her jacket and pulled out a small knife, the blade gleaming in the industrial lighting. She'd have one chance to cut Allegra free before the men noticed. After that, everything would depend on how quickly they could reach the exit.

Another explosion echoed through the building, this one shaking dust from the rafters above. The guards were shouting now, their voices getting closer as Enrico drove them back toward the main area.

"Time to go," Danny announced, pulling out a gun. "We take the girl with us."

"No," Riccardo said desperately. "If we leave now, we lose everything."

"If we stay, we die."

Danny moved toward Allegra, but Mishka was already in motion. She emerged from the shadows like a ghost, the knife cutting through the zip ties around Allegra's wrists in one smooth motion.

"Run," she whispered in Allegra's ear as she pulled away the blindfold.

But they were already too late. Danny had seen her, his gun swinging in their direction.

"We've got company!"

The gunshot was deafeningly loud in the enclosed space, but Mishka had already pulled Allegra behind a piece of machinery. The bullet sparked off metal inches from where they'd been standing.

"This way," Mishka said, pulling Allegra toward the service entrance.

But Riccardo was there ahead of them, his own gun drawn and pointing in their direction. His face was a mask of rage and desperation.

"You don't get to walk away," he snarled. "Not after everything you've cost me."

"Riccardo, don't do this," Allegra said, her voice steady despite the terror in her eyes. "You don't want to be a killer."

"Don't I? Because right now, killing you both seems like the only way to stop you talking."

More gunshots echoed from the front of the building as Nikolai engaged with the other guards. They were running out of time.

Dangerous Liaisons

"You think I don't know what you two are to each other?" Riccardo continued, his gun wavering between them. "You think I don't know about your perverted little affair? You have thrown insult and dishonour in my face."

"There's nothing perverted about our love," Mishka said quietly. "But there's everything wrong with what you're doing."

"Love?" Riccardo laughed bitterly. "You destroyed my life for love? My family, my future, my reputation—all for some dyke fantasy?"

"Riccardo—" Allegra started.

"Shut up!" The gun swung back to her. "You had everything. Everything I wanted, everything I needed. And you threw it away for her."

Mishka tensed, ready to throw herself between Riccardo and Allegra if necessary. But before she could move, another voice cut through the tension.

"Drop the weapon."

Enrico stood in the doorway behind Riccardo, his own gun trained on the younger man's back. His clothes were torn and dirty, but his stance was rock-steady.

"Drop it now, or I put a bullet in your spine."

Riccardo's hand shook, the gun wavering. For a moment, it looked like he might comply. Then his face twisted with rage, and he spun toward Enrico, bringing the weapon around.

Both men fired simultaneously.

Riccardo's shot went wide, sparking off a pipe overhead. Enrico's didn't.

Riccardo crumpled to the ground, clutching his shoulder and screaming in pain. His gun skittered across the concrete, well out of reach.

"It's over," Enrico said, moving to secure the weapon. "Danny and his boys are either dead or gone. I'm not sure which. Harbour patrol's on the way."

Mishka pulled Allegra into her arms, holding her tightly as the adrenaline finally caught up with both of them. Allegra shook, but she was alive and safe.

"Are you hurt?" Mishka whispered.

"No. Terrified, but not hurt." Allegra pulled back to look at her. "How did you find me?"

"I told you," Mishka said, her voice fierce with emotion. "We survive. Whatever it takes."

***

An hour later, they sat in the back of an ambulance while paramedics checked Allegra for injuries. Riccardo had been taken to the hospital under police guard, his shoulder wound serious but not life-threatening. Danny Torrino was in custody, and his two associates had disappeared into the night.

The police accepted that Riccardo had hired local criminals to kidnap Allegra for ransom, and that Enrico Castelli—cousin of the victim—had coordinated her rescue. Mishka allowed Enrico to bask in the limelight.

"Rico?"

They looked up to see Gianni Rossini approaching, his face drawn with worry and exhaustion. Behind him walked Volkov, equally grim.

"Papa," Allegra said, starting to stand.

"Stay," Gianni said gently, reaching out to touch her face. "Are you hurt?"

"I'm fine. Thanks to Rico and Mishka."

Gianni turned to Enrico, studying the younger man carefully. "Vincent Torrino called me. Told me what you did tonight. What you risked. I think he was covering his arse and protecting the Torrino's from retaliation."

"This was family. Anyone would have done the same."

"No," Gianni said firmly. "Not anyone. Many people would have called the police, let them handle it. You put yourself in danger to protect Allegra."

He embraced the younger man. "I owe you a debt," Gianni continued. "We'll talk in the morning about your role in the company."

Mikhail stepped forward as well, his pale eyes assessing his daughter with something that might have been pride.

"You did well tonight," he said simply. The words carried more weight than a lengthy speech.

Gianni turned to Mishka next. "And you, Ms. Volkov. Vincent told me you were instrumental in finding my daughter."

"I couldn't let anything happen to her," Mishka replied carefully. "She's... important to me."

Something flickered in Gianni's eyes—not understanding, perhaps, but awareness. He nodded slowly.

"The *Harbour Light* project," he said to Mikhail. "Perhaps we were too hasty in our disagreement."

"Perhaps we were," Mikhail agreed. "There's too much money at stake to let pride interfere with sound business decisions."

The two patriarchs shook hands, their feud officially ended. As they walked away to discuss details, Enrico moved closer to Allegra and Mishka.

"You two need to be more careful," he said quietly. "Tonight worked out, but there might be others who try to use your relationship against you."

"We know," Allegra said. "We'll prevent that by talking to our families ourselves. It's time. But thank you. For everything."

Enrico nodded and moved away, giving them a moment of privacy.

"So, what happens now?" Allegra asked.

Mishka's smile was tired but genuine. "Now we go home. Our fathers shake hands and pretend they never fought. The project moves forward, our families prosper, and we..."

"We what?"

"We survive," Mishka said, echoing her earlier words. "Together, whatever comes next."

As the ambulance doors closed and they were driven away from the pier, Allegra couldn't help but think that survival was just the beginning. The real challenge would be building a life together in the shadow of their families' expectations.

But as she felt Mishka's hand slip into hers, she thought they might just be strong enough to handle whatever came next.

Chapter 16

THE MORNING SUN streamed through the floor-to-ceiling windows of Gianni Castelli's office, casting sharp lines of light across the polished marble floor and the imposing mahogany desk that had served as both throne and battlefield for decades. The air smelled faintly of tobacco and leather—comforting and intimidating all at once. Allegra sat opposite her father, spine straight, heart thudding.

She couldn't delay this conversation any longer. Too much had changed. The events of the past weeks—the betrayal, the danger, the near-collapse of the consortium—had forced her to re-evaluate everything. Love had found her in the midst of it, unexpected and all-consuming. And now, it was time.

She took a breath. "Papa," she began, her voice steady despite the magnitude of what she was about to say. "We need to talk."

Gianni looked up from the stack of contracts he was reviewing. His gold cufflinks glinted in the sun, his expression unreadable. He studied her for a long beat, then set his pen down with deliberate care.

"Dimmi piccola" he said, his tone deceptively gentle. "Tell me."

"I'm in love with Mishka Volkov."

The words hung in the air between them like a live wire.

Gianni's eyes narrowed slightly, the only visible crack in his mask. "The Russian girl."

"Yes," Allegra said. She didn't flinch, didn't back down. "We're together. And we want to develop a project of our own."

His fingers began to drum against the polished wood—*tap, tap, tap*—a rhythm that once meant focus, but now sounded like a warning.

Gianni pushed his chair back and stood, pacing slowly to the window. He stood there, arms crossed, staring out over the city skyline like a general surveying a battlefield. When he finally spoke, his voice was quiet but hard.

"After everything that's happened? Riccardo. The threats. The whispers in the press. The... scandal."

Allegra stood too, facing him across the room. "*Because* of everything that's happened. Papa, I can't live my life in the shadows anymore. Not for the family. Not for appearances. I love her. And she loves me. She risked everything to protect me—what we have is real."

Gianni turned slowly, his face carved from stone. "Do you know how hard I fought to build this name? This legacy? And now you want to—what? Throw it all away for a... for *her*?"

"I'm not throwing anything away." Allegra's voice rose, passion breaking through restraint. "I'll keep my shares. I'll always be your business adviser. I'll always be a Castelli. But

Dangerous Liaisons

I want out of the day-to-day. I want something clean. Something Mishka and I can build on our own, without blood and secrets."

"You speak as if you're above all this," Gianni snapped, stepping forward. "As if you're not where you are because of the very empire you now want to walk away from."

"I *am* where I am because of this family," Allegra said, her tone fierce. "But I refuse to be swallowed by it. I won't become another pawn in a game I never agreed to play. Enrico is ready—he's been ready for years. He *wants* this life. Let him shadow you. Teach him. He should inherit this, not me."

Gianni's hands curled into fists at his sides. "And you think you can just walk away? You think the world outside these walls is cleaner? Safer?"

"No," Allegra said softly. "But I think it's *my life* to risk."

The silence that followed was heavy, taut. The only sound was the faint ticking of the antique clock on the shelf.

Then, slowly, Gianni moved back to his chair. He sat, not defeated, but older. More human.

"You are still my daughter," he said at last, voice thick. "That will never change."

Allegra's throat tightened. She stepped forward, placing her hand over his on the desk. "I know, papa. And you'll always be my father. But I need this. We need this. Mishka and I—we're not a phase. We're not a rebellion. We're a future."

He looked at her hand, then up at her face. His jaw clenched, a muscle twitching. "Does she love you?"

"Yes," Allegra said without hesitation. "And I love her. Enough to walk away from everything else."

Rowena Wylde

Gianni was quiet for a long moment. Then he nodded once—barely perceptible.

"Then you'd better make damn sure she's worth it."

Allegra smiled faintly. "She is."

***

That evening, Mishka's apartment overlooking Sydney Harbour glowed with candlelight. The city beyond the windows shimmered like a sea of scattered diamonds, the lights of ferries tracing slow arcs across the dark water. The occasional sound of laughter or music drifted in from the street below, but inside, the world had shrunk to just the two of them.

Mishka stood barefoot on the rug, wearing an oversized shirt that fell mid-thigh, sleeves rolled to her elbows. Her hair was still damp from the shower, curling slightly at the ends. Allegra had just finished lighting the last candle on the coffee table when Mishka slipped behind her and wrapped her arms around her waist, pressing a soft kiss to her shoulder.

"We did it," Mishka whispered, her breath warm against Allegra's skin. "We actually did it."

Allegra turned in her arms, eyes shining in the low light. "We did," she echoed, and kissed her—slow, lingering, full of disbelief and joy. But when she pulled back, a shadow crossed her expression.

"Are you sure about this?" she asked, her voice quieter now. "About us? About walking away from everything?"

"I've never been surer of anything," Mishka said, brushing Allegra's hair back behind her ear. "I love you,

Allegra Castelli. All of you—the fire, the ambition, the way you challenge everyone, including me."

Allegra exhaled a breath that trembled slightly. "Even the family complications?"

"*Especially* those," Mishka replied with a crooked grin. "Life with you will never be boring. And I've had enough quiet to last a lifetime."

Allegra laughed softly, shaking her head. "You're mad."

"Maybe. Mad about you." Mishka caught her mouth again, this time with more hunger, her fingers gripping the back of Allegra's neck like she didn't want to let go.

They moved to the couch, the wine on the table forgotten as they folded into each other, legs tangled, mouths eager. Between kisses, they spoke in fragments—half-thoughts and plans suspended between breathless laughs and hushed declarations.

"A boutique hotel," Allegra murmured against Mishka's neck. "Something intimate. Stylish. A place people remember."

"With a restaurant," Mishka added, her hands slipping under the hem of Allegra's shirt. "Nothing pretentious. Real food. Seasonal. Local."

Allegra tilted her head back, eyes half-lidded. "A courtyard. With jasmine and fairy lights."

"And a rooftop bar," Mishka said, her lips grazing Allegra's collarbone. "Where you can see the whole city. We'll build something beautiful together," Mishka pulled her closer. "Our name on the deed. Our rules. Our future."

Their kisses deepened, turning hungry, then desperate—tongues seeking, tasting, claiming. Allegra's fingers slid beneath the hem of Mishka's shirt, pushing it upward inch by inch, revealing smooth skin that glowed gold in the candlelight. Mishka raised her arms to let it fall away, and Allegra trailed her lips down the curve of her neck, across her collarbone, until Mishka was arching toward her with a breathless moan.

"God, you're beautiful," Allegra murmured, reverent and rough all at once.

Mishka reached for the buttons of Allegra's blouse with shaking hands, each one popping free under her fingers until the fabric slipped off her shoulders. Her mouth followed the trail—pressing hot, open kisses over Allegra's chest, her stomach, her hipbones—worshipping her, anchoring them both in the here and now.

They sank to the floor, tangled in cushions and silk. The rug beneath them was plush, but the only thing either of them felt was skin against skin, fire meeting fire. Allegra's thigh slipped between Mishka's, coaxing a cry from her lips that turned into a whisper of her name. Her nails grazed Allegra's back, urging her closer, deeper, until nothing existed but the rhythm of their bodies, the heat of each breath, the slick slide of limbs and longing.

Mishka rolled them over, taking control with a glint in her eyes, her mouth finding every inch of Allegra like she was memorizing her by touch. Every sigh and gasp was a kind of devotion, every touch a vow. They moved together with the kind of urgency that comes from too many close calls, too many secrets held behind closed doors.

"Stay with me," Mishka whispered against her ear. "All of you. Always."

"I'm yours," Allegra gasped, clinging to her. "I always was."

And when they came together, bodies shuddering in tandem, it felt like more than pleasure—it was release, and renewal, and a claiming of something sacred. The past burned away. Only the future remained, sealed in sweat and kisses and the fierce press of their joined hearts.

The next morning, sunlight spilled through the sheer curtains in soft golden stripes, painting the apartment in warmth. The air smelled of sea breeze, warm pastry, and fresh coffee.

Mishka padded barefoot from the kitchen, balancing two mugs and a paper bag that rustled with promise and a warm, tantalising smell. She wore one of Allegra's oversized shirts now, the sleeves falling past her hands, her hair still mussed from sleep and lovemaking. Allegra was already on the balcony, curled into one of the woven chairs with her legs pulled up beneath her, wrapped in a light throw.

Mishka nudged the door open with her hip and smiled as Allegra looked over her shoulder.

"You read my mind," Allegra said, reaching for the coffee.

"Years of Bratva training," Mishka said dryly. "We're taught to anticipate every need." She set the bag on the small table, revealing two warm croissants—flaky, golden, slightly crushed from the walk back but still perfect.

They ate in companionable silence for a while, the breeze lifting strands of their hair as they watched the morning unfold. Ferries crisscrossed the harbor, white wakes trailing behind them like signatures. Far off, the horizon shimmered blue and endless.

"This view never gets old," Allegra murmured, brushing a crumb from Mishka's lip with her thumb. "But it's not just the city I see this morning. I see… possibilities."

Mishka leaned her elbows on the balcony rail, cradling her coffee. "It's strange, isn't it? I've spent so much of my life looking over my shoulder. Watching the water for danger. Planning for the next fallout."

"And now?"

Mishka turned to her, eyes soft. "Now I'm watching it for what comes next. Not what I'm running from—but what we're running toward."

Allegra smiled, reaching out to slide her fingers through Mishka's. "We'll find our place. Not someone else's legacy, not a front for dirty money or a name we have to protect."

"Our name," Mishka said. "Our future."

The word *our* lingered between them like a benediction.

A seagull cried overhead, the scent of salt and coffee mingling with the promise of a warm day ahead. Allegra leaned her head on Mishka's shoulder, eyes half-closed.

"For the first time in a long time," she said, "I'm not afraid."

Mishka kissed the top of her head. "That makes two of us."

Dangerous Liaisons

They sat there for a while longer, watching the world move below them, steady and unstoppable—just like the life they were beginning to shape, one tender morning at a time.

***

Six months later

The Victorian mansion stood like a dowager empress fallen on hard times—its white paint flaking like old lace, windows boarded shut, the garden a wild tangle of weeds and stubborn roses. But as Allegra and Mishka stood at the rusted gates, wind lifting their hair and hope surging in their chests, they saw none of the decay.

They saw potential.

"It's perfect," Allegra breathed, her fingers closing tightly around the heavy iron keys the real estate agent had just handed over.

"It's a disaster," Mishka replied dryly, eyeing a cracked window pane—but her smile said otherwise. Her eyes glittered.

"Our disaster," Allegra said, and this time, Mishka nodded.

The purchase had drained the remainder of Allegra's trust fund and required a jaw-dropping loan from Mishka's grandmother, Sofia—who, to their astonishment, had produced substantial sum and a single, scrawled note.

"For my granddaughter's happiness," Mishka had translated, *"and to keep you both too busy to get into trouble."*

Now, standing before their dream made manifest in crumbling brick and grand bones, they felt the thrill of ownership, of risk, of possibility crackling in the air.

"*The Matilda*," Allegra said aloud, testing the weight of the words.

"It's perfect," Mishka replied. "This place will be for women. For escape. For power. For love." She glanced up at the vine-draped eaves, the elegant curve of the second-storey balcony.

Allegra grinned. "Simple. Strong. Unapologetic. I like it."

They moved through the empty house, voices echoing in rooms once filled with ballgowns and whispered gossip. The bones were solid—arched doorways, hardwood floors hidden under dust, a once-grand staircase that begged for restoration. A faded kind of elegance still clung to the place.

"This will be the restaurant," Mishka said, walking into the ballroom, now lit by slashes of afternoon sun. "Floor-to-ceiling windows, velvet banquettes, candlelight."

Allegra spun slowly, already seeing it in her mind's eye. "A menu built on fresh local produce. Wines from the region. No pretension—just heart."

"Upstairs," Mishka added, "twelve suites. Each one with its own name. Its own story."

Their phones buzzed simultaneously. They both glanced down.

Congratulations on your purchase. The Castelli and Rossini fathers have agreed to a truce. Don't make them regret it. – E

Allegra raised an eyebrow and showed her screen to Mishka. "Enrico?"

"Has to be." Mishka arched a brow, then promptly deleted the message. "Think they'll keep their distance?"

"They'll have to," Allegra said flatly. "We're not asking for permission anymore."

They stepped out onto the wrap-around porch as the sun began to set behind the Blue Mountains, streaking the sky in molten gold and bruised lavender. The house groaned around them—settling, waiting. Behind them stood history. Ahead of them, a future built with bare hands, grit, and ambition.

There would be battles: council red tape, structural surprises, staffing headaches, financial stress. But for the first time, it would be *their* battle. Their terms. Their empire.

"No regrets?" Mishka asked, her voice quiet as she slipped an arm around Allegra's waist.

Allegra leaned into her, anchoring herself in that strength. "Only that we didn't burn the old world down sooner."

"We didn't need to," Mishka said. "We just had to leave it behind."

Allegra smiled as the last of the sun dipped below the ridge. "Let them watch. Let them wonder."

"They'll know soon enough," Mishka said, her gaze sharp, her hand steady in Allegra's. "This is only the beginning."

And behind them, the house seemed to breathe in time with their pulse—rising from ruin, reborn into something fierce, feminine, and entirely their own.

***

Rowena Wylde

If you enjoyed reading Dangerous Liaisons, it would be helpful to future readers if you left a review for their benefit. They would appreciate it and I would be ecstatic.

You can do that by scanning this QR Code.

Or typing this address into your browser.

https://linktr.ee/rowenawylde

Rowena Wylde

Avenging Angel

She Hunts the Guilty. He Hunts Her.

Zahra delivers justice where the system fails. As an assassin for the Avenging Angels, she targets abusers who have escaped accountability. Silent, professional, and deadly, she leaves only a small angel figurine at each scene.

Detective Hamish Doyle is leading the hunt for the so-called Angel Killer. Under pressure to solve the case, he doesn't know that the woman who just walked into his life—and his bed—is the very person he's chasing.

When their separate missions uncover a dark network of exploitation and abuse, they must work together to take it down. But when the truth comes out, will Hamish turn her in—or let her go?

Plan B: Secret Donor Baby

Pyper always wanted a baby. The husband part? Optional. She skipped the fairytale, booked herself into South Coast Fertility Clinic, and took control of her future—thank you very much. A farewell fling with Charlie Jordan was just a victory lap.

Then—bam—six weeks pregnant and her dream job lands in her inbox. Obviously, she applies. She can hide a baby bump. She cannot hide ambition.

Beecham Constructions is everything she wants… except for one tiny complication: the Project Director is Charlie. Yes, that Charlie. Now she's juggling a secret pregnancy, a not-so-secret attraction, and a man who seems determined to keep things strictly professional—if only his attitude would cooperate.

Sharing a room wasn't her idea. Neither was falling for him. Just when Pyper thinks she's the only one with life-altering news, Charlie reveals a surprise of his own.

Rowena Wylde

Rowena writes in a seaside suburb in metropolitan Adelaide, South Australia. She loves writing stories that are character focused, but with a plot-line to entertain the reader. Her characters sometime surprise her with the things they say and do – it's always interesting to see what's happening on the next page.

Most of her stories are set in Australia, as that is the location she knows best. She welcomes readers from all over and delights in receiving messages from them in relation to her books.

She can be contacted via rowenawylde@gmail.com **Your reviews and feedback are always welcomed. https://linktr.ee/rowenawylde**.

You can join the mailing list to be advised of new releases at https://rowenawylde.com.au/mailing-list

Rowena Wylde

www.ingramcontent.com/pod-product-compliance
Lightning Source LLC
LaVergne TN
LVHW031540060526
838200LV00056B/4582